"WE HAVE
CONQUERED PAIN"

"WE HAVE CONQUERED PAIN"

THE DISCOVERY OF ANESTHESIA

DENNIS BRINDELL FRADIN

ILLUSTRATED WITH BLACK-AND-WHITE PHOTOGRAPHS

MARGARET K. McELDERRY BOOKS

For Judith Bloom Fradin, my wife and friend, with love

Consultant: David M. Rothenberg, M.D., Associate Professor and Director of the Division of Critical Care, Department of Anesthesiology, Rush–Presbyterian–St. Luke's Medical Center and Rush University of Chicago

Margaret K. McElderry Books
An imprint of Simon & Schuster Children's Publishing Division
1230 Avenue of the Americas
New York, New York 10020
Copyright © 1996 by Dennis Brindell Fradin
Book design by Virginia Pope
The text of this book was set in Life
Printed in the United States of America
First Edition
10 9 8 7 6 5 4 3 2 1

Library of Congress Cataloging-in-Publication Data
Fradin, Dennis B.
"We have conquered pain": the discovery of anesthesia / Dennis Brindell Fradin. — 1st ed. p. cm. Includes bibliographical references and index.
Summary: An account of the work of four doctors involved in the debate over the credit for use of anesthetics in the United States in the mid-nineteenth century.
ISBN 0-689-50587-6 (hardcover)
1. Anesthesia—History—Juvenile literature. 2. Jackson, Charles T. (Charles Thomas), 1805–1880—Juvenile literature. 3. Morton, W. T. G. (William Thomas Green), 1819–1868—Juvenile literature. 4. Long, Crawford Williamson, 1815–1878—Juvenile literature. 5. Wells, Horace, 1815–1848—Juvenile literature. [1. Anesthesia—History. 2. Long, Crawford Williamson, 1815–1878. 3. Wells, Horace, 1815–1848. 4. Morton, W. T. G. (William Thomas Green), 1819–1868. 5. Jackson, Charles T. (Charles Thomas), 1805–1880.] I. Title.RD79.F73 1996
617.9'6' 09—dc20   95-35538   CIP   AC

ACKNOWLEDGMENTS

For their help, the author thanks:

Dr. Shireen Ahmad, Assistant Professor, Department of Anesthesia, Northwestern University Medical School, Chicago, Illinois

Susan B. Deaver, Director, Crawford W. Long Museum, Jefferson, Georgia

Martin Bander, Michelle Marcella, and Peggy Slasman, Public Affairs, Massachusetts General Hospital

Diane Neumann, Librarian, Menczer Museum of Medicine and Dentistry, Hartford, Connecticut

Sally S. Graham and Patrick P. Sim, Librarians, Wood Library-Museum of Anesthesiology of Park Ridge, Illinois

Dennis Laurie, Assistant Curator of Newspapers and Articles, American Antiquarian Society

Ruth Hall and Stuart Hall, Mayflower Society, Plymouth, Massachusetts

Charles Berg, of Stamp King, Chicago

Charles Greifenstein, Historical Reference Librarian, College of Physicians of Philadelphia

CONTENTS

A NOTE FROM THE AUTHOR

What is the greatest invention or discovery ever made in the United States? Many people would choose the electric light, invented by Thomas Edison in 1879. Some would favor the polio vaccine Dr. Jonas Salk introduced in 1953. Others might say the automobile, the telephone, or the airplane. Yet most people would overlook a discovery that has saved hundreds of millions of lives: anesthesia.

Until the mid-1800s, doctors could not perform many operations now considered routine because they had no way to prevent pain during surgery. This was a major reason why people lived to an average age of about thirty-five in the early 1800s. Then in the 1840s anesthetics were discovered in the United States. As the news spread that doctors had found a way to put patients to sleep for surgery, anesthesia was hailed as "the greatest gift ever made to suffering humanity" and "the most valuable discovery ever made." The new process revolutionized medicine, for it meant that surgeons could operate on the internal organs without inflicting pain on their patients.

Only one other breakthrough in history has saved more lives than anesthesia. In the 1870s, Louis Pasteur of France and Robert Koch of Germany learned that germs cause disease. This discovery paved the way for scientists to create medicines that prevent and cure diseases. Together, the American discovery of anesthesia and the European discovery of the germ theory are the primary reasons why people in developed nations live to an average age of nearly eighty today.

"WE HAVE CONQUERED PAIN"

Left: Dr. Crawford W. Long (1815–1878) Born Danielsville, Georgia
Right: Dr. Horace Wells (1815–1848) Born Hartford, Vermont

Left: Dr. William T. G. Morton (1819–1868) Born Charlton, Massachusetts
Right: Dr. Charles T. Jackson (1805–1880) Born Plymouth, Massachusetts

A NOTE FROM THE AUTHOR

Four people were involved in discovering anesthesia: Georgia physician Crawford Long, Connecticut dentists Horace Wells and William Morton, and Boston chemist Charles Jackson. Each seeking credit for the discovery, the four men became embroiled in the most bitter medical battle in history—a battle that led to the insanity of one man and the deaths of two others. The United States Congress even became involved in the controversy, offering $100,000 to the discoverer of anesthesia, but withdrawing the reward when the lawmakers disagreed on who should receive it. The verdict of history has been similar to that of Congress. Tired of the bickering, the public gradually lost interest in the subject, so that today few people know anything about the origins of anesthesia.

As preparation for writing this book, I have visited numerous sites associated with the four men, and have examined records and journals dating back 150 years. My conclusion is that each of the men deserves at least partial credit for anesthesia. Certainly the many millions of us who enjoy the blessings of painless surgery sometime in our lives can find room in our hearts for four discoverers: Crawford Long, Horace Wells, William Morton, and Charles Jackson.

—DBF

*This woodcut from a 1517 book is one of the earliest
known pictures of an amputation.*

CHAPTER 1

TWO MILLION YEARS OF PAIN

Scene 1. The year is 1840, the place a doctor's home. Early in the morning a man raps on the door with trembling knuckles. From the look of terror on his face, one might think he is about to be tortured. This is basically the case, for he has come for an operation.

Appearing nearly as upset as his patient, the doctor leads him into the "operating room," actually just a specially equipped room of his house. "This will help," says the doctor, offering a glass of whiskey. After two glassfuls the patient relaxes a little, but when the doctor asks him to lie on the table, he is overcome by such dread that he tries to run away. The doctor has prepared for this. Two burly assistants waiting nearby grab the patient and strap him down to the table.

The patient watches in horror as the surgeon takes his scalpel, chisel, saw, and clamp from a drawer. "Please, no!" he cries, pulling like a wild animal at the straps. For the next few minutes the poor man feels indescribable pain as the surgeon cuts through his skin and then probes with his tools.

Scene 2. The time is the present, the place a hospital operating room, where a woman is about to have cancer surgery. The woman had thought she would be terrified, but now she is eager to be rid of her tumor. The anesthesiologist injects medication into the intravenous catheter (tube) that has been placed in the patient's arm. As the woman begins to lose consciousness, the anesthesiologist reassures her that she will be fine. Once she is asleep, the operation begins. She remains asleep during the entire procedure, completely unaware that the surgeon is removing her tumor.

After the operation, the patient is taken to the recovery room, where she receives medication through her catheter to control her postoperative pain. The next day, with her family around her bedside, she learns from her doctors that the operation was a success. She tells her anesthesiologist that she remembers nothing about the operation, and has had a minimal amount of pain.

Analysis of ancient human bones proves that people have suffered disease and pain ever since human life appeared on Earth two million years ago. Cancer, arthritis, and a host of other diseases afflicted the ancients just as they plague us today. Our prehistoric ancestors made the first attempts at treating some of these ailments surgically. Ancient skulls with holes cut in them have been found around the world. Called trephination, this earliest kind of surgery involved cutting a piece out of the skull with a flint knife. The ancients seem to have done this to let out the demons that they thought caused disease. Trephination was painful, so the prehistoric surgeons probably experimented with plants and other substances found in nature in the hope of discovering ways to reduce the agony. We have no knowledge of these experiments, however, for *prehistory* means the time before written records.

Written history has been kept for only about five thousand years. Ancient writings contain many references to painkilling substances. Wine, made from grapes, and opium, made from

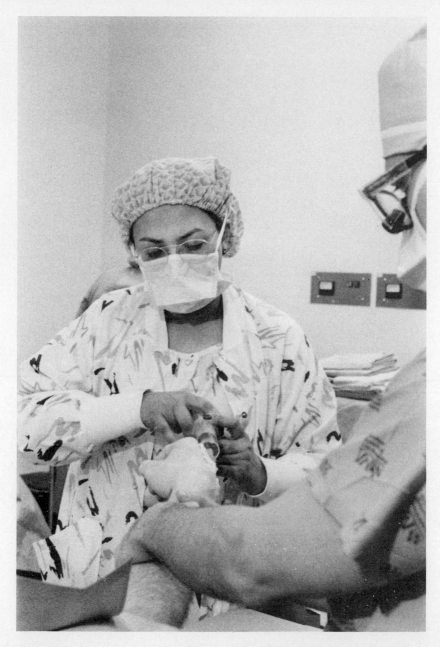

*A present-day anesthesiologist injecting medication into a
surgery patient*

the opium-poppy plant, were two of the earliest known and most widely used of these substances. The Greeks believed that the roots of mandrake plants had magical qualities, including the ability to put a person to sleep. They also believed that when pulled from the ground the plant let out a cry that could kill a person, so they had dogs dig up mandrake. Nearly two thousand years ago, the Greek physician Dioscorides used mandrake potions, which he claimed "produced anesthesia," on surgical patients. This was the first known use of the word *anesthesia,* which is Greek for "without feeling," referring to a drug's ability to prevent pain.

Doctors in India and China used marijuana and hashish, both made from hemp plants, to relieve surgical pain. Galen, a great doctor of the Roman Empire, made a sleep-inducing medicine out of the bitter milky juice of lettuce. The North American Indians used the jimsonweed plant to make an anesthetic. Indians in South America used certain plants to make curare, a drug that paralyzed a person when it entered the bloodstream.

The one quality all the ancient anesthetics shared was that they didn't work well. Each violated at least one of the three major attributes of a good general anesthetic (a drug used for producing unconsciousness in a surgical patient). The drug must block pain; it must be able to put a patient to sleep and keep him or her asleep throughout an operation; and the drug must not be harmful. Curare, for example, did not prevent pain and could kill the patient by paralyzing the breathing muscles. Marijuana was too weak to put a patient to sleep, as was also true of Galen's lettuce anesthetic.

The Greek Hippocrates is often called the Father of Medicine. To this day, graduating medical students repeat the famous Hippocratic Oath, in which they promise to work "for the benefit of the sick." Hippocrates and his followers compiled about one hundred medical books, yet they made no mention of anesthesia. It appears that beyond giving surgical patients wine, Hippocrates and most ancient doctors considered the quest for a reliable anesthetic hopeless.

During the Middle Ages (A.D. 400–1500), little progress was made in any of the sciences. This period of European history is often called the Dark Ages because science seemingly moved backward in many ways. There was a widespread feeling that to search for scientific explanations was an affront to God. An astronomer who claimed that the Earth went around the sun instead of vice versa faced being put to death, as did a doctor who examined dead bodies to seek the cause of disease.

The Middle Ages were especially dark in the field of medicine. One epidemic after another ravaged humanity, claiming huge death tolls. The black death, a bubonic-plague epidemic that struck between 1330 and 1350, killed 75 million people and at times seemed about to wipe out the human species. Had they examined the evidence, people might have realized that bubonic plague was carried by fleas from infected rats. Instead, people blamed epidemics on demons, mysterious vapors, and unlucky alignments of the planets.

Strange remedies were concocted to combat illness. It was a Europeon custom to bake a gingerbread cake in the shape of a sick person, which was then given to a beggar. The demon causing the illness was supposedly transferred through the gingerbread person from patient to beggar. Sick people of the Middle Ages also wore charms around their necks containing the word *abracadabra* (origin unknown), which supposedly could cure them. Children still eat gingerbread people and magicians still say "Abracadabra!" without knowing the background of these customs.

Scientists and alchemists who continued the search for anesthetics created some strange concoctions, too. A formula from the 1200s called for coal tar to be mixed with wax from a dog's ear. It was claimed that a patient who swallowed this mixture would sleep for four days. Soap, eaten instead of used for bathing, was another would-be anesthetic of the Middle

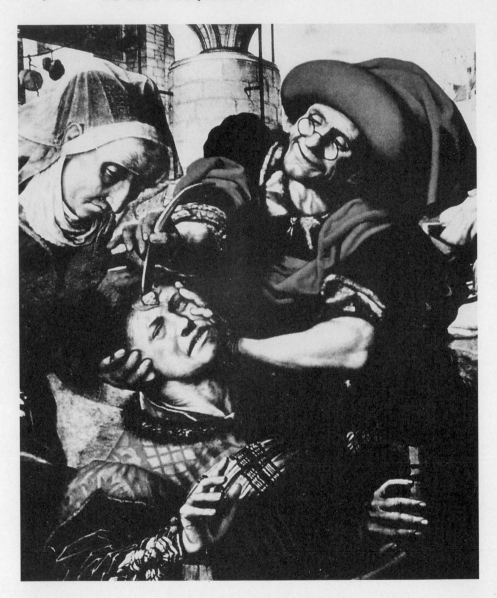

A surgical operation of the 1500s

Ages. But the most popular anesthetic of the time was the *spongia somnifera* (Latin for "sleeping sponge"). This was a kind of anesthetic stew, containing such substances as mandrake root and mulberry and hemlock juice, that was placed on a sponge and held to the patient's nose. A twentieth-century scientist who tested one *spongia somnifera* recipe concluded that "it couldn't put a guinea pig to sleep."

Although this is far from certain, it is believed that in 1275 Raymond Lullus, a Spanish physician and philosopher, was experimenting when he produced a colorless, sweet-smelling liquid. Lullus apparently had no idea of the anesthetic powers of what he called sweet vitriol, later named ether.

Nearly three hundred years later, Theophrastus Bombastus von Hohenheim, known as Paracelsus, continued where Lullus had reportedly left off. Born in Switzerland during the 1490s, Paracelsus practiced medicine there and in many other lands. Although he had remarkable success at treating patients, Paracelsus was kicked out of town after town because he questioned such ancient medical authorities as Hippocrates and Galen. Paracelsus even publicly burned old medical texts, proclaiming that rather than relying on past ideas, scientists must seek "the deepest knowledge of things themselves and of nature's secrets" by experimenting. In one of his many experiments, Paracelsus exposed chickens to sweet vitriol. The results deeply impressed him. "It is taken even by chickens, and they fall asleep from it for a while but awaken later without harm," he wrote. Paracelsus added that sweet vitriol "quiets all suffering without any harm, and relieves all pain."

Paracelsus was a towering figure of the Renaissance (French for "Rebirth"), a period of renewed interest in learning that lasted roughly from the late 1400s to around 1600. He might have made the greatest discovery of the Renaissance had he given a surgical patient sweet vitriol, but he didn't, perhaps fearing that he would be condemned to death for using so potent a drug. Following Paracelsus's death in 1541, humanity had to wait another 301 years for the first successful operation under anesthesia.

Scientists continued to experiment with sweet vitriol without appreciating its true value. In 1730 the German chemist Frobenius gave sweet vitriol a new name. He called it *ether,* a word from the Greek meaning "heavenly."

In 1772 the English scientist Joseph Priestley discovered nitrous oxide, a gas that would figure prominently in anesthesia. For nearly thirty years little experimentation was done with nitrous oxide, for it was thought that breathing even a small amount would cause death. Then in 1798 nineteen-year-old Humphry Davy was hired as an experimenter at the Pneumatic Institution at Clifton, England, where patients were treated by being given various gases to breathe. Davy read that breathing nitrous oxide would kill a person, but because he had doubts, he decided to take Paracelsus's advice and experiment.

Most scientists start with animals before experimenting on humans, but Davy reversed the order. One spring day in 1799 Humphry Davy breathed nitrous oxide himself. Instead of dying, he began laughing, so he nicknamed nitrous oxide "laughing gas." Davy then put a cat, rabbits, and other animals safely to sleep with laughing gas. His main subject continued to be himself, however. "Whenever I have breathed the gas," he noted, "the delight has been often intense and sublime." Soon he craved the happy feeling the gas created and was breathing it regularly. Davy wrote poems and went on moonlit walks while inhaling the gas, shocking bystanders with his half-conscious laughter.

Perhaps because he began with the honest intention of testing the substance, we can excuse Humphry Davy for becoming a laughing-gas addict. His experience also illustrates that once begun, drugs can seize hold of anyone, even a great scientist. Later, two and perhaps three of the four main dis-

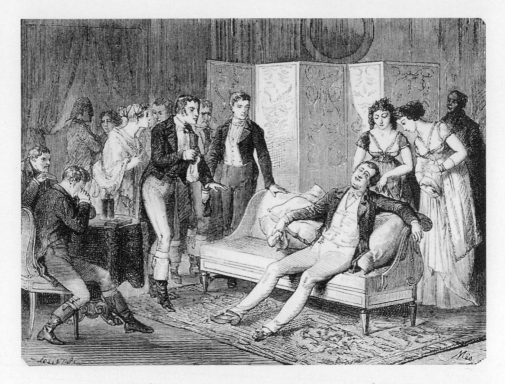

Humphry Davy experiencing a bizarre reaction after
breathing nitrous oxide

coverers of anesthesia would have similar experiences, but with far different outcomes.

In 1800 Davy published *Researches, Chemical and Philosophical, Chiefly Concerning Nitrous Oxide.* He wrote that nitrous oxide "may probably be used with advantage during surgical operations." Had he actually given nitrous oxide to a patient undergoing an operation, Davy would probably be hailed as the discoverer of anesthesia today. But, like Paracelsus, he neglected to take that crucial step.

Humphry Davy's craving for laughing gas was a passing episode in his life. He overcame his addiction and went on to make many chemical discoveries. He became a hero to miners for inventing the Davy lamp, which reduced the chances of explosions in coal mines. Davy also discovered six of the approximately one hundred elements that make up our universe. As his fame grew, Davy looked back on his laughing-gas studies with embarrassment, and regretted writing about the subject. Little did he realize how close he had come to a discovery that would have dwarfed his other achievements.

One more scientist came close. In the same year that Davy published his book on nitrous oxide, Henry Hill Hickman was born in England. Henry decided upon a medical career as a child, after seeing an accident in which a workman was badly hurt. He became a doctor and surgeon who treated poor people for free, but he couldn't stand the pain his knife caused those he wanted to help.

By his early twenties, Hickman was experimenting with ways to put animals to sleep for surgery. One method he tried was to deprive them of air. This was dangerous, for if air is taken away too long, the patient will die. Next he put animals to sleep by having them breathe carbon dioxide. This wouldn't work well for people either, for we exhale carbon dioxide and cannot survive by inhaling it without air.

Still, Hickman was on the right track. Some historians claim that he went even further by putting animals to sleep with nitrous oxide, and that he may even have done anesthesia experiments on people. Whether or not these claims are true, Hickman certainly might have become the discoverer of anesthesia with a little encouragement and a few more years of life. He was granted neither.

In 1824 Hickman wrote *On Suspended Animation*. He sent this booklet, which was the first separate work ever published on anesthesia, to the prestigious Royal Society of London. A few words of praise from its president, and Hickman's scientific career would have been launched. But Humphry Davy—who had been knighted as Sir Humphry Davy in 1812—was the society's president. Hickman's work reminded Davy of what he considered his own misspent exper-

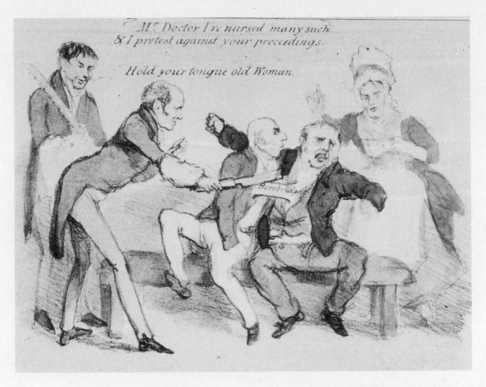

This cartoon makes fun of doctors' helplessness to do
surgical operations; the doctor is separating Siamese twins.

iments of a quarter century earlier. Sir Humphry and other leading scientists in England ignored Hickman.

Henry Hill Hickman then went to France, where he tried to interest doctors in his experiments. There, too, the young scientist was ignored. Dr. Hickman returned to England, where he died a short time later at the age of thirty. Thus, in 1830, humanity was little closer to the great discovery than it had been three centuries earlier.

CHAPTER II

ETHER FROLICS AND LAUGHING-GAS PARTIES

The scene now shifts three thousand miles westward across the Atlantic Ocean to the United States. If we could travel back to the 1840s, we would find a far different nation from the one of today. First, there weren't nearly as many people. The United States population in 1840 was 17 million—one-fifteenth its current total. Then, as now, New York was the largest city, but in 1840 it had only 313,000 people—one twenty-fifth as many as today.

Despite the smaller population, families were much larger in 1840 than they are now. Typically a woman married at sixteen, had six children by the age of twenty-five, and more than one hundred great-grandchildren by the age of seventy-five—if she lived that long. People in the United States lived to an average age of about thirty-five in 1840. Mothers commonly died in childbirth, and epidemics killed thousands of people at a time, especially the young, so that a family with twelve children could expect to have only six reach adulthood.

The causes of disease were a mystery to the doctors of the 1840s. Back in the 1670s Anton van Leeuwenhoek of the

Netherlands had seen what he called "wretched beasties" through his microscope, but not until the late 1800s would scientists realize that these bacteria, as they became known, cause disease. Ignorant of the existence of germs, doctors of the 1840s commonly worked all day without washing their hands. As a result, those who were supposed to heal were among the biggest spreaders of disease.

There were no antibiotics or other "miracle drugs" yet to treat pneumonia and other diseases. Pharmacology—the field of making and dispensing medicines—wasn't even a science yet. Still, there was no shortage of medicines. Anyone could concoct secret remedies called patent medicines and sell them, for no laws regulated the making of drugs. Apothecaries (as druggists were called), doctors, and ordinary citizens created "wizard oils" and other medicines. These were often sold in traveling "medicine shows," which also featured singing and other entertainment.

People believed that if a medicine was foul enough, it would drive away the disease. Does your child have whooping cough? Step right up and buy a bottle of Mephitis Putorius (the spray of a skunk mixed in alcohol). A sheep-dung soup was a remedy for the measles, and a bath in liquor mixed with hot human urine was prescribed for people who couldn't stop trembling. The famous Boston doctor and writer Oliver Wendell Holmes once said that people would be better off if all the known medicines were thrown into the ocean, only it would be a disaster for the fish.

Anyone needing serious heart, brain, or intestinal surgery in 1840 was as good as dead. Amputations of limbs, removal of tumors close to the skin, and operations for bladder stones were performed, but since the pain of these operations could be deadly, too, "the quicker the surgeon, the greater the surgeon" was the rule of the day. Besides a stopwatch, bottles of liquor were another necessity in the operating rooms of the 1840s, for alcohol was the only anesthetic then in use.

Surgeons were known to enter the operating room with a bottle of whiskey in each hand—one for the patient and the other for the doctor so that he could endure his patient's screams.

Many operations believed to be successful ended in the patients' deaths later. Again, germs were the problem. Surgeons wore the same smocks week after week and even joked that a coat wasn't broken in until it could stand up by itself from all the dried blood. Germs from the surgeon's clothing and hands often made their way into patients' bodies and killed them.

To make things worse, most Americans of the 1840s had toothaches. The main qualification to become a dentist was enough strength to pull teeth quickly. But since even the fastest dentists could not prevent pain, people commonly preferred a mouthful of rotting teeth to having them extracted. Dentists were widely viewed with disdain, for it was their practice to advertise "secret methods" that more often than not failed to live up to their billing.

Their teeth hurt. They died young. And yet the Americans of the 1840s knew how to have fun. Rural people held country fairs. Punch and Judy puppet shows traveled about, as did circuses that displayed such creatures as lions and elephants. "Flying men" (acrobats) came to town to swing from the highest steeple.

Phineas T. Barnum was one of the first to capitalize on the American people's hunger for the unusual. In 1841 he opened Barnum's American Museum in New York City. There, and in touring shows, Barnum displayed curiosities. Some were genuine, such as the midget known as General Tom Thumb, but others, such as the "mermaid" that was actually a fish attached to a monkey, were what Barnum called "humbugs."

Taking P. T. Barnum's advice that Americans didn't mind paying to be "humbugged," many traveling "professors" charged people to see their "scientific demonstrations." Palm

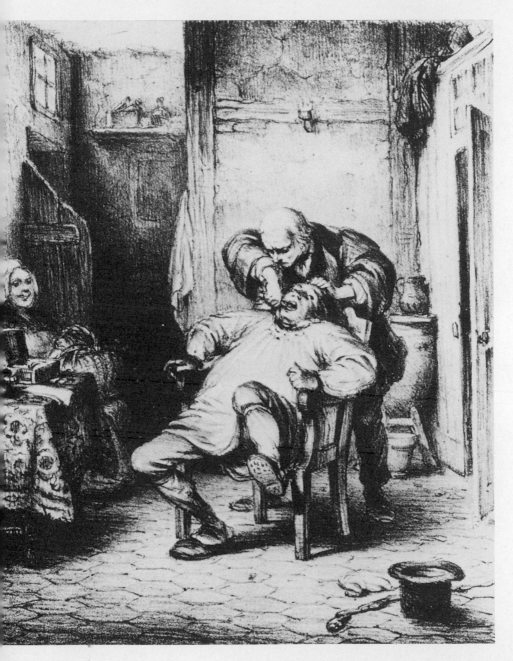

A dentist of long ago

readers saw the future in peoples' hands, mind readers revealed thoughts, phrenologists analyzed personal traits through the bumps on peoples' heads, and spiritualists put people in touch with the dead—always for a fee, of course.

Not all the traveling professors were humbugs. Unlikely as it seemed, mesmerists could actually place people in a trance-like state. Around 1842 this process became known as hypnotism. A few surgeons of the time hypnotized patients and told them that they wouldn't feel the knife. Hypnotism actually did help reduce pain, but generally only in less-serious operations.

One group of traveling showmen played a key role in the development of anesthesia. By the 1830s Humphry Davy's dis-covery that people acted silly under the influence of laughing gas was well known. "Chemical lecturers" packed containers of laughing gas onto horse-drawn carts, then went from town to town presenting "nitrous oxide demonstrations" at fairs, tent shows, and meeting halls.

The typical admission charge for a "chemical lecture" was twenty-five cents. After the audience plunked down its Miss Liberty quarters and was seated, the professor emerged from behind the curtain. Science, he explained, had discovered a substance with the remarkable ability to transform those who inhaled it. A few of the professor's assistants breathed the gas from silk bags and suddenly became very jovial, dancing and performing acrobatics across the stage. Once the handful of demonstrators quieted down, the professor presented a scien-tific lecture about the gas—just to remind everyone that they were there for educational reasons. Next came the highlight of the show. Would a few volunteers step onto the stage and breathe the gas? Always a few hearty souls did so in the inter-est of science.

Soon the hall was rocking with laughter. The mayor—gen-erally the picture of dignity with his muttonchop whiskers, tailcoat, and silk stovepipe hat—breathed the gas and began

A cartoon from England mocking the laughing-gas craze;
these men are giving their wives nitrous oxide.

doing somersaults. The village blacksmith danced across the
stage like a ballerina. The schoolmaster thought that his cane
was a bat in the new sport of baseball.

At the end of the show, the professor explained that the
next day there would be a lecture for ladies only. He added
that, for a fee, people could have private demonstrations in
their homes or even buy their own supply of laughing gas.

Around 1840, the use of laughing gas as well as ether
spread among the general public. Since the country had no
drug-abuse laws yet, there was nothing but their own good
sense to prevent people from misusing these substances,
which sometimes caused death. Many people refused to have
anything to do with the drugs. Thousands of others across the
nation obtained laughing gas and ether from town chemists
and traveling professors, then held "laughing-gas parties" and
"ether frolics." These gatherings became especially popular

among students at academies (which were similar to our high schools) and at colleges. In fact, under the guise of scientific study, medical-school professors routinely gave their students ether and laughing gas. Often the students continued to inhale these drugs in their rooms after class. Countless people must have bruised themselves without feeling the pain while cavorting around under the influence of laughing gas and ether. Yet not until a young doctor from Georgia made an interesting observation did these substances begin to take their rightful place in medicine.

CHAPTER III

"DOCTOR SAVIOUR"

Jefferson, located in a cotton-growing area of northeast Georgia, was one of many towns where laughing-gas parties were popular in the 1840s. With about five hundred people counting its outskirts, Jefferson was a bustling town for its time and place. The county courthouse, the Jackson County Academy, and two stagecoach inns stood on the town square. Downtown Jefferson also included two blacksmith shops, three wagon makers, a lawyer's office, eight stores, and the home and office of a young physician.

The doctor, Crawford Williamson Long, was born in Danielsville, twenty miles from Jefferson, on November 1, 1815. His two-story boyhood home, still standing in Danielsville, was one of the area's finest houses. Crawford's father was a cotton planter, state senator, and postmaster, and he also owned a dry-goods store in Danielsville. As the family's wealth grew, so did their number of slaves—from two when Crawford was four years old to nineteen a few years later.

The large library was one of Crawford's favorite spots in his boyhood home. When Crawford was five years old, his parents

Crawford Long's boyhood home in Danielsville, Georgia

discovered him reading the Bible aloud. He went on to read his parents' old Shakespeare editions and other books. Crawford also spent many hours horseback riding and hunting in the nearby woods, and fishing and swimming in the area's streams.

After Crawford became famous, his family related a story about the first "operation" he performed. Five-year-old Crawford and his three-year-old sister Sarah thought up a game to play with a hatchet. They took turns holding a hand on a wooden block, moving it at the last instant as the other swung down the hatchet. One time, Sarah waited too long, and Crawford severely cut three of her fingers. Crawford held his sister's bleeding fingers in place while their mother applied sugar to help heal the cuts and then bandaged the hand. Fortunately, all of Sarah's fingers were saved.

Upon completing his studies at Danielsville Academy, fourteen-year-old Crawford enrolled at the University of Georgia in Athens, a town that, with Jefferson and Danielsville, forms a triangle with twenty-mile sides. In those days college students were all male and generally younger than they are today. Still, fourteen was an early age to be entering college even in 1829. Crawford was assigned to room with Alexander H. Stephens, later the Vice President of the Confederacy during the Civil War. Since Stephens was four years older than Long, their classmates called them Daddy and the Baby.

"The Baby" joined the Demosthenian Society, a debating and literary club, at the university. Somewhat like a modern fraternity, the Demosthenians had their own hall, where they gave speeches and held debates. The group also fined members for infractions of rules. Crawford Long was once fined fifty cents for "sleeping in the hall." He had a far more serious run-in with the college officials. Frances Long Taylor, whose biography of her father provides much of our information about him, wrote that he had witnessed "some prank which his friends had played." Officials demanded that he tell what he knew, but he remained silent even when threatened with expulsion. In the end he was not expelled, but his loyalty prevented him from graduating with highest honors.

Now nineteen years old, Crawford told his parents that he wanted to become a doctor. The Medical College of Georgia in Augusta was one hundred miles away, and apparently his mother and father wouldn't yet allow him to go that far from home. The family reached a compromise. Crawford would begin his medical education by studying under and assisting Dr. George Grant in Jefferson. During his time with Dr. Grant, Crawford lived with his sister Sarah, who had married the lawyer with the office on the Jefferson town square. Besides studying medicine in Jefferson, Crawford also served as principal of Danielsville Academy, his boyhood school.

When Crawford was twenty-one, his parents finally let

him leave Georgia to attend Transylvania University in Lexington, Kentucky, which had one of the nation's best medical schools. In 1836 he rode about four hundred miles on horseback through the mountains to the university, where he attended medical lectures for a year. For his second-year course of lectures he transferred to the University of Pennsylvania in Philadelphia, where the students inhaled ether and laughing gas for recreation. Reportedly Crawford first did this with friends in a Philadelphia boardinghouse.

Crawford earned his medical degree from the University of Pennsylvania in 1839. He then went to New York City, where he spent a year and a half "walking the hospitals"—going about to the various hospitals and treating patients. He specialized in surgery, and earned a reputation for his speed and skill. His ambition was to become a navy surgeon and travel the world, but Crawford was still the dutiful son. When his parents objected, he returned home.

Actually, Dr. Crawford Long settled twenty miles from his parents' home. Dr. George Grant, his teacher in Jefferson, was moving to Tennessee. Crawford paid one thousand dollars for Dr. Grant's home and the office next to it on the town square. And there, shortly before his twenty-sixth birthday on November 1, 1841, Crawford Long settled.

More than a sense of duty drew him back to Georgia. During a visit to Jefferson after his graduation from the University of Pennsylvania, Crawford saw a girl named Caroline Swain, and was so captivated that he decided to marry her. Caroline was just fourteen at the time, however—two years from the traditional marrying age for women. As he settled into his medical practice, Crawford had only weeks to wait before Caroline turned "sweet sixteen" in December of 1841.

The life of a country doctor was more difficult than Crawford Long had expected. He mixed his own medicines, packed them into his saddlebags, then visited his patients in all kinds of weather at all hours, often far from home. His transportation was a big gray horse named Charley. One event

Crayon portrait of Crawford Long at age twenty-six

Dr. Long later related to his children was the time he had trouble prodding Charley across a bridge on a stormy night. Only later did Long realize that the usual bridge had been replaced by a temporary structure intended for lighter weights. Charley had saved him from plunging into the river, so from then on Long gave his horse the reins in the dark, letting him decide the best route.

Now and then Dr. Long performed simple amputations, removed cysts and tumors on or near the skin, and took out bladder stones, but surgery was rare in his country practice. Delivering babies became his favorite kind of work and his specialty. During his nearly forty years as a doctor, Crawford

Long delivered hundreds of babies and had only two mothers die of complications—a remarkable record for the 1800s.

Upon settling in Jefferson, Long resumed his friendship with many people he had known from his earlier years there. His office became a gathering place for Jackson County Academy students and other young men of the town. On evenings when there were no medical emergencies, Long and his friends met in his office to talk and play checkers, chess, and the card game called whist. At one of these sessions, his friends asked Dr. Long if he could supply them with some laughing gas. Long had no apparatus for preparing nitrous oxide, but he supplied them with ether instead.

The young physician joined in his friends' ether frolics, which began in December of 1841. Dr. Long noticed that as he and his friends stumbled about after inhaling ether, they often banged into the furniture or fell to the floor without seeming to feel any pain. "Didn't you feel that?" he repeatedly asked his friends. "They uniformly assured me that they did not feel the least pain from these accidents," he later reported.

James Venable, a Jackson County Academy student around twenty-one years old, was one of the men who participated in these ether frolics. Venable wanted to be rid of two small tumors on the back of his neck, and spoke to Dr. Long several times about an operation. Yet each time Long set a date, Venable changed his mind for fear of the pain.

One day as Long watched his etherized friends bump into things, it occurred to him that surgical patients might be put to sleep with ether so that they could undergo painless surgery. It seems like an obvious conclusion, and Long himself later said, "The mystery is that it was not discovered long before." Yet often in science the obvious is overlooked until someone with imagination comes along.

On March 30, 1842, Long told Venable his idea. "We have received bruises while under the influence of ether without suffering, so probably an operation could be performed under

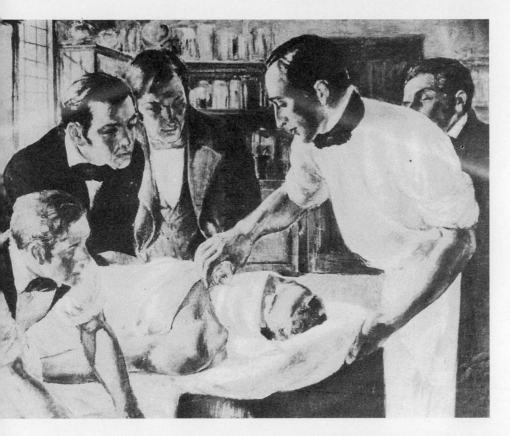

Artist's version of Crawford Long's hlstoric operation on
James Venable

its influence without pain." As an added inducement, Long
offered to perform the operation for two dollars—including
the ether—instead of the usual rate of forty dollars for removal
of a tumor. Venable agreed to have Long cut out one of the
tumors that very evening.

Two of his classmates at the Jackson County Academy and
the school's principal came with James Venable to Crawford
Long's office. Long sat Venable in a chair, then poured some
ether on a towel, which he placed under the patient's nose.
After a short time, Venable slumped into his friends' arms. He

did not stir during the entire operation. In fact, the surgery was noteworthy for its lack of drama. Instead of shouts of pain, there was silence. Instead of the patient begging for the cutting to stop, he dreamed on, his rhythmic breathing and the pulse in his neck the only signs that he was alive. The operation was over in a few minutes and the towel was removed from under Venable's nose.

James Venable was disappointed when he awoke, for he thought the operation hadn't yet begun. Only when Dr. Long held up the half-inch tumor did Venable realize the surgery was completed. Crawford Long made a simple entry in his account book: "James Venable, March 30, 1842, Ether and Exsecting Tumor, $2.00."

Long's operation on James Venable was the first in history using a true anesthetic. But science requires something more of a discoverer than being first. The primary dictionary definition of *discover* is "to make known," which is precisely what science demands. The breakthrough must be made known to the greater world so that everyone can benefit.

Had the operation occurred in New York, Philadelphia, New Orleans, Charleston, or Boston, the news would have spread to all corners of the Earth with no effort from Long. If Samuel Morse's telegraph were not merely in its infancy, Long might have sent out the news to a big city that very night. But it would be another two years before the nation's first telegraph line opened. As it was, Long's best way for publicizing his breakthrough would have been to write an article like the following for a medical journal:

> The first patient to whom I administered ether in a surgical operation was Mr. James M. Venable, who then resided within two miles of Jefferson, and at present lives in Cobb County, Georgia. Mr. Venable consulted me on several occasions in regard to the propriety of removing two small tumors situated on the back part of his neck, but would postpone from time to time having the operations per-

formed, from dread of pain. At length I mentioned to him the fact of my receiving bruises while under the influence of the vapor of ether, without suffering, and as I knew him to be fond of, and accustomed to inhale ether, I suggested to him the probability that the operations might be performed without pain, and proposed operating on him while under its influence. He consented to have one tumor removed, and the operation was performed the same evening.

The ether was given to Mr. Venable on a towel; and when fully under its influence I extirpated the tumor. It was encysted, and about half an inch in diameter. The patient continued to inhale ether during the time of the operation: and when informed it was over, seemed incredulous, until the tumor was shown him. He gave no evidence of suffering during the operation, and assured me, after it was over, that he did not experience the slightest degree of pain from its performance. This operation was performed on the 30th March, 1842.

Long actually *did* write the above description, but not until 1849 for the *Southern Medical and Surgical Journal*. He had some bad luck in regard to this journal, which was published in Augusta in his home state and was the logical place for him to present his discovery to the world. Published from 1836 until 1839, the *Southern Medical and Surgical Journal* was then discontinued, and didn't resume until 1845. A similar misfortune in timing occurred at Transylvania University's medical journal, another likely place for Long to publish an article. The *Transylvania Journal of Medicine* appeared from 1828 to 1839, then was discontinued for a decade, and didn't appear again until 1849. Still, there were other medical publications in existence, such as the *New England Journal of Medicine*. For a century and a half, people have wondered why Long didn't write an article about his historic operation for one of these journals.

One possible answer that has been presented is that Long hated to write and kept putting it off. Yet at this time he was writing long letters to Caroline Swain, who was now staying with family friends twenty-five miles from Jefferson. Just three weeks after the Venable operation, Crawford wrote Caroline a letter in which he related his dream about "imparting a kiss on your beautiful cheek." Crawford courted Caroline for several months following her sixteenth birthday, and on August 11, 1842, they were married.

Another excuse made for Long was that he was too busy to write an article. An incident at his wedding illustrated how busy he was. On the evening of the ceremony, Long wasn't at the church on time. After a while a few people headed for home, assuming he had backed out of the marriage. Actually, Dr. Long was with a very sick patient whom he felt should not be left alone. He finally managed to slip away for the ceremony, but then rushed back to spend the night with his patient. Not until the following morning did he return to his bride. "The doctor is so absorbed in his professional duties that I see but little of him," Caroline wrote in her journal of their first year of marriage. Still, there must have been a few hours now and then when he could have written an article.

When Long finally published his article on ether anesthesia in December 1849 he anticipated the big question. "Why did I not publish the results of my experiments in etherization soon after they were made?" he wrote. "I was anxious, before making my publication, to try etherization in a sufficient number of cases to fully satisfy my mind that anesthesia was produced by the ether, and was not the effect of the imagination, or owing to any peculiar insusceptibility to pain in the persons experimented on." Everyone who knew Crawford Long vouched for his honesty, so we can take him at his word that a desire to make sure the method was reliable was the original reason for his delay in publishing.

Between the historic March 1842 Venable operation and his December 1849 article, Dr. Long did a handful of other operations using ether. In June 1842 he removed the second growth from James Venable's neck. Later he amputated a diseased toe of a slave boy, removed a growth similar to Venable's from a woman's head, and amputated another slave boy's finger. In each case the anesthetized person reported feeling no pain during surgery.

Dr. Long also found another use for ether. Over a twenty-year period Crawford and Caroline had twelve children —seven girls and five boys. For the birth of their second child, Frances, Crawford eased Caroline's pain by having her breathe ether. However, Frances would never reveal her age, not even in her biography of her father, which came out in 1928 when she was eighty-two. As a result, for many years it was thought that the Scottish doctor James Simpson became the first person to use an anesthetic in delivering a baby in January 1847. Only when Frances's birthday was publicly revealed to be December 17, 1845, following her death at age eighty-four, did historians realize that Crawford Long was the first doctor to use an anesthetic in childbirth. Dr. Long later administered ether to other women during childbirth.

Why did Long continue his silence after his additional successes? Frances writes that despite her father's growing reputation, a few people considered him a kind of Dr. Frankenstein, the scientist in Mary Shelley's 1818 novel *Frankenstein*, who makes a monster out of dead bodies. These people believed that God intended humanity to suffer pain and that preventing it was the devil's work, sure to end in disaster. Frances briefly discussed the threats to her father she had heard about as a girl:

> He was considered [by some people] reckless, perhaps mad. It was rumored throughout the country that he had a strange medicine by which he could put people to sleep and carve them to pieces without their knowledge. His friends pleaded with him to abandon its use as in case of a fatality he would be mobbed or lynched [hanged].

Add to this the fact that many people associated ether with naughty parties and show business, and we can see why he was reluctant to draw attention to his work by writing an article.

Meanwhile, as the years passed, Long became a beloved figure in northeast Georgia far beyond Jefferson. If a patient didn't have the money, he accepted farm crops in payment of a bill. Dr. Long also provided free medical care for poor whites as well as slaves. At times he traveled to distant plantations to deliver babies of slave women and to treat sick slaves. The black people of the region appreciated his care so much that they called him "Doctor Saviour."

Crawford Long was also blessed with a very happy home life. He and his wife doted on their twelve children, six of whom lived to adulthood. Even at eighty-two, Frances remembered the warmth of her family's life seventy-five years earlier. Toward the end of each day, Caroline and the children would look out the window in hope of seeing Crawford approaching on Charley. In the evening, Crawford helped the children translate their Latin and do their mathematics. Later they all sat playing checkers or reading books and magazines. From his Transylvania University days, Long remembered the beautiful horses in Kentucky's Bluegrass region. He imported Kentucky horses for the family carriage, and bought each of his children a pony as soon as they were old enough to ride.

It is interesting to imagine what a hero the young Georgia physician would have become had he written just a short article about his ether work around 1843. Crawford Williamson Long would be a household name today, there would be schools named for him across the nation, and his birthday (the day after Halloween) might be a holiday. But Dr. Long remained silent, opening the way for others to claim the discovery and adding a few more years to the many centuries of surgical pain.

CHAPTER IV

"HUMBUG" OR "THE GREATEST DISCOVERY EVER"?

The anesthesia story now moves one thousand miles north to New England, the region in the nation's northeast corner comprising Massachusetts, Maine, Vermont, New Hampshire, Rhode Island, and Connecticut. Although all six states together are little larger than Georgia, New England led the nation in its early years in many ways. The Revolutionary War that gave birth to the United States began in New England, as did the country's public school system. Furthermore, New Englanders such as William Lloyd Garrison led the fight against slavery, while others, including Susan B. Anthony, directed the struggle for women's rights.

New Englanders were so inventive that a phrase was coined about it: "Yankee ingenuity." In 1816 Samuel Read Hall, a teacher in Maine, created the nation's first school blackboard. Samuel Morse of Massachusetts invented the telegraph in 1837. With the help of money he earned demonstrating laughing gas, Connecticut's Samuel Colt developed his famous Colt six-shooter in the 1830s. The hundreds of other inventions by New Englanders range from chewing gum to doughnuts.

Despite their achievements, New Englanders were widely viewed by other Americans as moneygrubbing and pushy. People claimed that Connecticut salesmen who traveled about with pushcarts were so crafty that they sold fake nutmegs (a spice) made of wood; this is why Connecticut is called the Nutmeg State. New Englanders also had a way of dismissing the accomplishments of other regions. Even today most Americans think that the permanent settlement of the thirteen colonies began when the Pilgrims landed at Massachusetts's Plymouth Rock in 1620. Actually, the settlement of Jamestown, Virginia, in 1607 marked the beginning. Southerners would later claim that the Yankees' habit of grabbing every "first" robbed their own Crawford Long of his rightful place in history.

At the time that Dr. Long performed the first painless surgery on James Venable, a dentist named Horace Wells was practicing in Hartford, Connecticut. Dr. Wells had a penchant for towns named Hartford. He was born in Hartford, Vermont, on January 21, 1815—the year of Crawford Long's birth—in a big wooden house that is still there. In 1820 the family moved to Bellows Falls, Vermont, where his father set up the region's first gristmill (a device for grinding grain) and smut mill (a device for ridding grain of unwanted material). Contact with this machinery may have inspired Horace's life-long interest in mechanical devices.

Horace's well-to-do parents sent him to a number of fine private schools and academies in Massachusetts and New Hampshire. But when Horace was fourteen, his father died. Besides suffering the crushing loss, Horace had to start making his own way in the world. While pondering his future, he taught penmanship in several schools. He thought about entering the ministry, but because of his mechanical aptitude his family decided he should become a dentist.

For two years Horace studied with dentists in Boston.

Horace Wells's birthplace in Hartford, Vermont

Then, when his teacher-dentists said he was ready—abracadabra—he was a dentist. At twenty-one, Wells set up practice in a larger Hartford than his birthplace—the capital of Connecticut. The handsome young man with red hair and blue eyes soon became famous around Hartford for, as his newspaper advertisements proclaimed, his "Improved Method of Filling Teeth" and for "inventing a set of Instruments for FILLING TEETH, which supersede those in common use." Within weeks of opening his office on Main Street, Horace wrote his sister Mary that "I am here happy as a clam—firing away at teeth," and that "my profits are from about 5 to 20 dollars a day." Quickly his income rose to one hundred dollars a week—a fortune for the time.

Actually, Horace wasn't "happy as a clam." His letters to his *Dear, Dear, Dear* Sister" Mary make it clear that he missed his family and felt very lonely in Hartford. He provided Mary with a touching story about how he entertained himself with his pet birds. "All the family that I have," he wrote her in 1837, "is 3 canary birds and one French Linnet [a kind of finch] which sings sweetly. I have now a splendid accordion and when I commence playing, the birds commence singing so we have fine concerts." In a letter to his mother at Thanksgiving time, he asked her to send him a drumstick from the holiday turkey, or save it until he was able to visit her.

In 1838 Horace's social life improved when he met Elizabeth Wales. Everyone who knew Horace described him as sensitive and shy, but the second adjective didn't apply to his romance with Elizabeth. Horace began by writing her a letter asking if she would consider marrying him. Elizabeth responded that she would have to know him better before she could decide. Soon they were courting at Elizabeth's house in Hartford. Four months later, Elizabeth Wales became Elizabeth Wells. The twenty-three–year-old groom built a cottage for his bride and himself in Hartford about half a mile from his office. When the couple had been married a year, Elizabeth gave birth to their only child, a son named Charles.

Wells's professional life continued to blossom. Around the time that he married, he published a book entitled *An Essay on Teeth*. His reputation achieved such heights that Connecticut governor William Ellsworth and his wife employed him as their dentist. Wells also found time to invent various contraptions, including a shower in which the bather pumped the water with his feet and a machine for keeping people who worked with coal from being coated with the dust.

Dr. Horace Wells

The prosperous young dentist began to take on students, including William T. G. Morton, who was just four years younger than Wells, and who became his friend. Their relationship became even closer in 1843 when Wells invented a gold solder to hold artificial teeth in place. Wells and Morton decided to become partners in Boston, Massachusetts, where they hoped to win fame and fortune using the gold solder. Wells's plan seems to have been to spend a few weeks in Boston setting up the new practice before moving Elizabeth and their son there. Wells and Morton opened the office as planned, and showed Horace's invention to Dr. Charles T.

Jackson, a renowned Boston scientist. On October 28, 1843, Horace wrote to Elizabeth with some exciting news:

> We have also succeeded in getting the certificate of the most celebrated chemist and geologist in the country in relation to my invention which will undoubtedly secure a first rate business to the office. His name is Dr. C. T. Jackson which you have undoubtedly heard of before, he expressed himself in the highest terms of admiration respecting the improvement, and he spent 3 days in analyzing the gold to see if it was as it appeared to be; he has made his report in writing and has given us permission to publish it, which we shall do next week. Any statement coming from such an eminent man must have a wonderful effect....

Despite Dr. Jackson's help, the solder did not catch on as Wells and Morton had hoped; nor did the Wells-Morton partnership work out, perhaps because Horace was too homesick to give it time to get going. After only about two weeks, Wells pulled out of the partnership and returned to Hartford.

Over the next year, Wells's success in Hartford continued. But one aspect of his profession deeply troubled him: His tooth pulling and other dental work inflicted enormous pain on his patients. Perhaps what frustrated him most was that he had a gift for inventing, yet there seemed to be no hope of finding a way to prevent pain—until the day that he noticed the following advertisement in the *Hartford Courant*:

> A GRAND EXHIBITION of the effects produced by inhaling NITROUS OXIDE, EXHILARATING or LAUGHING GAS! will be given at UNION HALL, THIS EVENING, Dec. 10th, 1844.
>
> FORTY GALLONS OF GAS will be prepared and administered to all in the audience who desire to inhale it.
>
> TWELVE YOUNG MEN have volunteered to inhale the

Gas, to commence the entertainment.

EIGHT STRONG MEN are engaged to occupy the front seats, to protect those under the influence of the Gas from injuring themselves or others. This course is adopted that no apprehension of danger may be entertained. Probably no one will attempt to fight.

THE EFFECT OF THE GAS is to make those who inhale it either Laugh, Sing, Dance, Speak or Fight, etc., etc., according to the leading trait of their character. They seem to retain consciousness enough not to say or do that which they would have occasion to regret.

Horace and Elizabeth Wells were in the crowd that paid twenty-five cents apiece to enter Hartford's Union Hall the night of December 10, 1844. "Professor" Gardner Colton, who had gone out on the laughing-gas circuit at the suggestion of P. T. Barnum, was the lecturer. Colton gave a talk on nitrous oxide, then the TWELVE YOUNG MEN who were part of the show inhaled the gas and began stumbling and dancing across the stage. When the professor asked for volunteers, Horace Wells shocked Elizabeth by rising from his chair. She tried to stop him, but he was determined to experience the gas's effects.

Once on the stage, Wells inhaled the gas with the other volunteers. Soon they were leaping and dancing about, but Wells's mind was clear enough to observe something. While under the influence of the gas, Samuel Cooley, a young drugstore clerk, smashed his legs on a bench very hard. Blood oozed through his pants, yet he did not cry out or show any other sign of pain.

When they returned to their seats, Wells pointed to the blood on Cooley's trousers. "You must have hurt yourself," Wells said. "No," Cooley answered, astonished to find his legs so bloody. Wells closely watched Cooley and saw that he felt no pain until the effects of the nitrous oxide wore off.

As the crowd filed out of Union Hall, Horace Wells approached Professor Colton to introduce himself. The fact that

Colton, like Wells, was a Vermont native helped them become fast friends. "Why cannot a man have a tooth extracted under the gas, and not feel it?" Dr. Wells asked Gardner Colton. The professor answered that he did not know. Wells then said he thought it could be done and arranged for Colton to meet him at his office the next day with a bag of nitrous oxide gas.

Horace Wells was so excited that he stayed up nearly all night discussing the possibility of using laughing gas in tooth pulling with John Riggs, a former student who had become a dentist. At the time, Wells had a troublesome wisdom tooth. He decided that he would inhale the laughing gas and then have Dr. Riggs pull the tooth.

The next morning, Gardner Colton came to Wells's office with the laughing gas. Wells sat in his own dental chair and placed the rubber tube leading from Colton's bag of nitrous oxide into his mouth. The plan was for Wells to breathe far more of the gas than people did at the "lectures," for he was to go beyond the usual stage of silliness into complete unconsciousness. As Dr. Riggs later recalled, "We knew not whether death or success confronted us. It was a *terra incognita* [unknown land] we were bound to explore."

Wells soon closed his eyes, and Riggs placed the forceps inside his mouth. Riggs gripped the tooth, rocked it back and forth to loosen it, then yanked it from the bone. When Wells opened his eyes, he stared in amazement at the wisdom tooth that Riggs proudly held up for him to see.

"I felt it no more than the prick of a pin!" shouted Wells. "It is the greatest discovery ever made!" He wanted to rush out and tell the world that he had just planned and been the patient in the first known removal of a tooth under an anesthetic. But, like Crawford Long, Horace Wells realized that the scientific way was to test the method on a number of patients before publicizing his discovery.

Wells had Colton tell him everything he knew about laughing gas before the professor left Hartford. Over the next

*Dr. John Riggs holding up the tooth for the awakening
Dr. Wells to see.*

several weeks, Wells and Riggs administered laughing gas to about a dozen patients in Hartford and then performed dental surgery on them.

Nervous even in normal times, Wells became increasingly excited as patient after patient reported that their dental work had been painless. Soon he could barely eat or sleep. Elizabeth Wells later recalled how her husband would suddenly bolt from the supper table and run to his office to try another nitrous oxide experiment. Then at night he would lie in bed pondering ways to present his discovery to the world.

Wells decided that he must do a major demonstration in Boston. If he successfully demonstrated his technique in "the hub of the solar system," as Dr. Oliver Wendell Holmes called the Massachusetts capital, the news would radiate as fast as ships and trains could carry it to every corner of the planet.

In January of 1845, Horace Wells returned to Boston, where William T. G. Morton had remained to practice dentistry and attend Harvard Medical School following the breakup of their brief partnership. Morton had come to know many of Boston's prominent doctors, and he and his wife boarded with Dr. Charles T. Jackson, who had helped promote the dental solder Wells had invented. Through Morton, and possibly with Jackson's help, Horace Wells was introduced to the nation's leading surgeon.

Meeting Dr. John Collins Warren was a thrilling but frightening experience for Horace Wells. The sixty-six–year-old surgeon had many achievements to his credit. In 1812 he had helped begin the *New England Journal of Medicine,* and in 1821 he had founded Boston's Massachusetts General Hospital, which was associated with the Harvard Medical School. So great was Warren's reputation when Wells met him in early 1845 that a few words from him could launch or ruin a career.

But praise, or even a smile, was rare from Dr. John Collins Warren, who was famous for his brusque, sarcastic manner and somber image. Like a number of people before him, Horace Wells asked Dr. Warren if he could come to the hospital to demonstrate his method for preventing pain. Warren had not found hypnotism or any other method he had witnessed satisfactory, and held little hope that the Hartford dentist would succeed. Yet Warren was willing to give a grudging chance to almost anyone who claimed to have a new technique. Yes, Horace Wells could present his demonstration following one of Warren's lectures.

On January 20, 1845, a short news item about Horace Wells appeared in the Boston *Bee*: "A dentist in Hartford, Connecticut, has adopted the use of nitrous oxide gas in tooth pulling. It is said that after taking this gas the patient feels no pain." The exact day of Horace Wells's demonstration is unknown, but it was sometime around January 21, 1845, his thirtieth birthday. Wells brought William Morton with him to a hall near Massachusetts General Hospital on the appointed

Dr. John Collins Warren

evening, where they waited with their bag of nitrous oxide and dental tools while Dr. Warren finished his lecture.

The high-strung Wells was in a state of near hysteria by the time Warren was ready for him. The fact that the doctors and medical students in the audience viewed dentists with contempt added to his anxiety. Dr. Warren cut Wells down further with an icy introduction. "There is a gentleman here," said Warren, "who pretends he has something which will destroy pain in surgical operations. He wants to address you. If any of you would like to hear him, you can do so." Warren's words

Horace Wells's famous "failure" to anesthetize a patient

set the audience to snickering, as intended, but nearly everyone remained in the lecture hall in anticipation of seeing the
Hartford dentist fail.

Wells told the audience what he had learned about laughing gas. Although he hadn't brought a patient, he knew that a
number of people in any group needed dental work. Was anyone in the audience willing to have a tooth pulled under
laughing gas?

A young man stepped forward, and Wells sat him in a
chair. With Morton's assistance, Wells administered the gas to
the patient. When he fell back in the chair asleep, the audience
stopped snickering. Horace Wells opened the patient's mouth,
clutched the tooth with the dental forceps, and pulled. As the
tooth came out, the patient groaned or cried out. Horace Wells

later blamed himself, saying that he "removed the gas-bag too soon." The moment the patient exhibited discomfort, the students and doctors began hissing and shouting "Humbug!" and "Swindler!"

Devastated by what had happened, Horace Wells fled the lecture hall. The people in the audience were so busy laughing and hooting that they did not realize the demonstration had actually been a success and the failure was theirs. For had anyone asked the patient, he would have explained, as he did later, that he had "felt practically no pain." But the patient was ignored and the students went off to amuse themselves by— ironically—inhaling laughing gas! Was there ever a better example of Paracelsus's comment to his fellow doctors three centuries earlier: "This is the cause of the world's misery, that your science is founded upon lies. You are not professors of the truth, but professors of falsehood...."? "Wells's failure," as it came to be known, meant two more years of pain for surgical patients, and paved the way for the next chapter in the anesthesia saga.

CHAPTER V

"GENTLEMEN, THIS IS NO HUMBUG"

The day after his demonstration, Horace Wells left Boston. He returned to Hartford, where he continued to give nitrous oxide to his own dental patients. About forty Hartford-area people later testified that Dr. Wells performed dental work on them using laughing gas soon after his Boston demonstration. Claiming that the use of laughing gas "should be as free as the air we breathe," Wells generously shared his technique with other Hartford dentists. By mid-1845, nitrous oxide was in wide use among dentists in the Connecticut capital.

If Wells had published an article in 1845 or had invited the Boston doctors to witness his successes in Hartford, he might still have been hailed as the discoverer of anesthesia. But, like Crawford Long, he remained silent. The reason in Wells's case is easier to determine. He was too despondent over his "failure" to continue promoting his cause.

Wells's feeling that he had missed the great opportunity of his life seems to have resulted in a mental breakdown. In April of 1845 he turned his practice over to Dr. John Riggs and temporarily retired from dentistry. Wells wrote that "the excitement of this adventure [the Boston demonstration] brought on an illness from which I did not recover for many months, being thus obliged to relinquish entirely, my professional business."

To help himself recover, Wells went into a completely different kind of work. First, he arranged "Wells's Panorama of Nature," which he presented at Hartford's City Hall. The Panorama may have been a kind of museum exhibit that included birds, rocks, plants, and fossils. Wells then seems to have put together a show featuring singing canaries. He traveled around Connecticut with the birds, perhaps playing his accordion while they sang.

Neither the Panorama nor the singing birds earned Wells much money, yet they temporarily revived his spirits. After five months' retirement, he resumed his dental practice. But Wells had grown too restless to stick to anything for long and he gradually drifted away from dentistry again. This time he and a partner formed a business to make and sell the foot-pumped shower bath Wells had invented. Wells traveled around trying to sell the device in New England and New York, but his partner tried to take advantage of him, and in November of 1846 Wells pulled out of the business. Around this time his former partner Dr. Morton made his own bid for recognition as the discoverer of anesthesia.

William Thomas Green Morton was born on August 9, 1819, in Charlton, Massachusetts, forty-five miles southwest of Boston. His birthplace was a small farmhouse with a big stone chimney. Morton's family was not wealthy. In fact, of the four claimants for the discovery of anesthesia, Morton grew up in the most modest circumstances. Yet he was not born into poverty, either, for in the 1800s families with roofs over their heads who raised their own food and sewed their own clothing did not consider themselves poor. The Mortons' apple orchard provided them with fruit and cider. They also grew beans, potatoes, and pumpkins to eat, while their sheep

William Morton's boyhood home in Charlton, Massachusetts

provided wool for their clothing.

William's parents wanted him to become a doctor. "To be a doctor is to be somebody and to have a respected place in the community," his father often said. Knowing of William's ambition, his friends nicknamed the boy "the doctor." William even concocted medicines out of plant roots that he had his relatives and friends swallow. This once nearly ended in tragedy. Apparently William used unripe elderberries or some other poisonous part of the elder tree to create a medicine that he poured down his sister's throat. The little girl nearly died, and "the doctor" was forbidden to make medicines afterward.

When he was eight, William Morton began school—really just a shack run by a farm girl who could barely read. His parents were so intent on his going to a better school that when he was twelve they moved into town to be near the Charlton

Academy. But teachers came and went there, so his father then enrolled William at the nearby Oxford Academy, arranging for him to board with a family friend named Dr. Pierce.

Excited to be living with a genuine physician, young William spent many hours reading Pierce's medical books. He also pestered the doctor until he took him along on patient visits and let him roll bandages. William's schoolwork suffered at the expense of his interest in medicine, but worse problems lay ahead. When William had been at the academy for about a year, another boy accused him of violating a school rule. The teacher ignored William's claims of innocence and demanded that he apologize.

William Morton was as high-strung and sensitive as Horace Wells, but while Horace fled difficult situations, William's impulse was to fight it out. Still proclaiming his innocence, he talked back to the teacher. In his life story, *Trials of a Public Benefactor,* dictated to an author many years later, Morton said that the teacher then inflicted an "outrageous punishment" on him, probably whipping him. Worse still, William was expelled from Oxford Academy.

William returned to Charlton, where his family had bought a store. He went to work behind the counter, selling cloth, coffee, and fish, but by his own admission he was "unfit for thought and action over several months." His health was broken and he was very moody and upset. When he wasn't needed in the store, he wandered the hills and woods, brooding about how he had suffered for the sake of his honor.

After a few months at home, William was sent to Northfield Academy, fifty miles away. There, under the guidance of a young science teacher named Dr. Wellington, he explored the countryside, collecting minerals and identifying birds. But William was unbearably homesick at Northfield Academy, which was a six-hour coach trip from Charlton. Soon he persuaded his parents to transfer him to Leicester Academy, closer to home. His classmates there later remembered that while they played games during free time, William went off alone to study nature. Yet in his quiet way, young Morton was happy during his two years at Leicester Academy. He planned to finish there and then attend medical school—until the day he received an urgent message to come home immediately.

Once there, he learned that his family had suffered a financial disaster. The family store had failed and his father was in debt. William's parents had to withdraw him from school and sell their property to pay what they owed, which meant that they could not return to farming as a means of support. William Morton later recalled, "I was there [at Leicester Academy] when the news of the failure of my father—utterly unexpected by his family—reached me and ended my school education. My father lost all his property, our family were scattered, and for several years had no home together."

The Mortons had connections with a few people in Boston's publishing industry. Seventeen-year-old William obtained a job as office boy for the *Christian Witness* magazine and moved in with the editor and his wife. Willie, as people began calling him, also worked for a time for Sarah Josepha Hale, editor of the *Ladies' Magazine* and author of the children's rhyme "Mary Had a Little Lamb." Mrs. Hale later remembered Morton as an intensely ambitious young man. "I knew Willie Morton as a clerk in the publication office of my magazine," she recalled. "Morton did not think merely about [earning a] living as most would." He had dreams of doing something great in the world, she explained—something that would result in the "improvement and essential advancement" of humanity.

To obtain funds for medical school, Morton invested his salary in business deals in Boston. We lack details, but somehow his business acquaintances took advantage of his innocence and youth to cheat him out of his money. He then settled upon dentistry as his stepping stone to medical school. In 1840 Morton went to Baltimore, where the world's first dental school was just being founded. Although it is not clear

Dr. William T. G. Morton

that he actually attended the Baltimore College of Dental Surgery, he did study with Dr. Horace Hayden, one of the school's founders, perhaps as a private student. By 1841 Morton was a student of another Horace—Dr. Wells of Hartford.

In 1842, twenty-three–year-old William Morton set up practice in Farmington, Connecticut, ten miles from Wells's Hartford office. Tall, distinguished-looking, and well trained, Dr. Morton nonetheless had trouble attracting patients at first, and for a time couldn't afford his own lodgings or dental tools. He had to sleep on a couch in his office and borrow tools from his former teacher, Dr. Wells.

One day Morton attended a dance at the Elm Tree Inn in

Farmington, where he met sixteen-year-old Elizabeth Whitman. Afterward, he wrote in his diary that he would marry Elizabeth one day. But nothing came easily to William Morton, including winning Elizabeth Whitman's hand. The prominent Whitman family objected to a poor dentist courting their daughter. However, Morton promised that dentistry was just the start of his career, that he was going to enter Harvard Medical School once he had enough money. There was another reason that the Whitmans allowed Morton to continue to court their daughter: Elizabeth loved him. Soon Elizabeth and William made a pact that when his career was a little further along, they would marry.

Morton's dental practice began to flourish after that. In 1843 Horace Wells created the gold dental solder, and thought of his ex-student as just the man to make it a success. Wells and Morton moved from Connecticut to Boston, where they set up practice at fashionable 19 Tremont Row. Morton immediately began to promote the solder, obtaining the certificate from Dr. Charles T. Jackson. Although the solder enterprise was a failure and Wells soon returned to Hartford, Morton remained in Boston, where he built up a large practice, began attending lectures at the Harvard Medical School, and studied as Dr. Jackson's private medical student. Jackson and his wife liked Morton so much that they had him come live with them in their large house on Boston's Beacon Hill.

Impressed that Morton was living and studying with the renowned Dr. Charles T. Jackson, the Whitmans finally gave their blessing to the marriage of Elizabeth and Morton. The ceremony, which took place in May of 1844, was described in a letter Horace Wells wrote to his mother:

> I attended his wedding at Farmington a few weeks since…. He has married a fine girl…. According to his story he is making $18,000 a year…. I know he is making money fast for he keeps two workmen employed beside himself, but

when he talks about making $18,000 a year I am apt to think he is using his tongue in making a random statement which he is no stranger to....

After the wedding, his bride moved in with William Morton at the Jackson house. Elizabeth was amazed by how hard her husband worked at his dental practice and medical studies. Each morning he arose between four and five to do what he called his "serious work," meaning his medical reading. William also kept a tall skeleton in a big box near the head of their bed, and Elizabeth often awoke to find him examining the bones.

One day when Morton had been married a few weeks, he asked Dr. Jackson if he knew any way to deaden pain in dentistry. Jackson said that when pulling teeth as a physician, he had given patients ether "toothache drops"—not to breathe, but applied to the gums to diminish the pain. Morton began using Jackson's toothache drops to numb teeth in the summer of 1844. He used them on a Miss Parrott, and perhaps on Jackson's aunt, whom the doctor brought to Morton for extensive dental work. Morton wondered whether he could not only lessen pain but prevent it altogether and he searched for clues in Dr. Jackson's books about ether and other painkilling substances.

In December, Horace Wells attended "Professor" Colton's lecture and began his nitrous oxide experiments. Wells then visited Morton to obtain his assistance for his demonstration at the hall near Massachusetts General Hospital. After his infamous "failure" in Boston, Wells retreated from his anesthesia experiments. Morton, however, was just about to begin his.

Besides all of his other activities, Morton was a volunteer preacher at his church, resulting in his and Elizabeth's repeated lateness for Sunday dinner. One spring Sunday in 1845, Jackson flew into such a rage over their tardiness that the Mortons moved out of his house. To at least remain on speaking terms with Jackson, Morton sent him a traveling bag as a good-bye present. On a large piece of land in what is now

Wellesley, outside Boston, Morton built a house for Elizabeth and himself and a cottage for his parents.

His estate at Wellesley became known as Etherton because of the experiments Morton did there. Wells's work with laughing gas, the ether frolics of the time, and Jackson's toothache drops and books combined to inspire Morton to change the direction of his life. He turned his Boston practice over to a friend, Dr. Grenville Hayden, then began experimenting to see if ether could put patients to sleep for dental surgery.

Morton began with animals. He caught goldfish in the pond at Etherton and tried to anesthetize them, but they were poor subjects since fish lack lungs. Elizabeth Morton later related that "he used to bottle up all sorts of queer bugs and insects, until the house was full of crawling things. He would administer ether to all these little creatures, and especially to the big green worms he found on grape vines." These, too, were poor subjects, but he succeeded at etherizing birds and then decided to proceed to something closer to a human being.

Morton's father had a reddish brown water spaniel named Nig who kept William company as he worked in his laboratory at Etherton. One day Morton placed Nig's head in a jar of ether and kept it there until the dog wilted in his arms. However, the dog had breathed too much ether and remained unconscious for so long that Morton feared he was dead. Fortunately, Nig finally opened his eyes, stood up, and walked on wobbly legs toward the house, where Elizabeth asked what had happened.

"Poor Nig," said Morton. "I've had him asleep a long time. I was afraid I had killed him."

"Do you put the fish asleep, too?" Elizabeth asked.

"I try to," her husband answered, "but have not succeeded yet." William must have sensed that his wife was poking fun at him. "The time will come, my dear," he added, "when I will banish pain from the world."

But Elizabeth Morton was also worried about her husband. "I was only a girl of eighteen," she later recalled. "I only

Dr. Morton and his family at Etherton

knew that his clothes seemed always saturated with the smell of ether, and I did not like it."

One day when Morton was trying to etherize Nig again, the dog broke free and knocked over the jar. Morton saved what was left of the ether and decided that he had experimented on animals long enough. He took the ether jar to his old office in Boston the next day. There he poured the ether onto his handkerchief, sat down in a chair, and inhaled the fumes until he drifted into unconsciousness. When he awoke, he rushed over to one of his former assistants.

"I have got it now!" Morton excitedly told him. "I shall take my patients into the front room and extract their teeth, and then take them into the back office, put in a new set, and send them off without them knowing anything about the operation!"

Morton realized that more tests were needed on human subjects. He obtained another supply of ether and asked Dr. Grenville Hayden to inhale it. Hayden refused. Next he asked his two former assistants, one of whom had taken part in ether frolics at school. The two young men agreed, but instead of falling asleep, both began yelling and jumping about and had to be restrained until their excitement passed. Morton was befuddled. Why did the first batch of ether put Nig and himself peacefully to sleep while the second batch failed with the two assistants?

Morton now saw that he had been wise to remain on speaking terms with Dr. Jackson, who, as one of the country's leading chemists, would know the answer. Talking to Jackson would be tricky, though, for Morton felt so close to a discovery that he wanted to keep his work to himself. He especially wanted to keep it secret from Jackson, who had a history of claiming other people's discoveries.

On September 30, 1846, Morton visited Dr. Jackson at his Beacon Hill home. He asked to borrow a gasbag, making Jackson think he was planning to give patients laughing gas, not ether. "Well, Doctor, you seem to be all equipped, minus the gas," Jackson said, providing Morton with a gasbag. Then Jackson warned, "You had better not attempt such an experiment, lest you be set down as a greater humbug than Wells."

Seeing his opening, Morton asked, as though it had just occurred to him, "Why cannot I give ether gas [instead of laughing gas]?" Jackson answered that he had witnessed the Harvard students' ether frolics, and that he thought ether might put patients to sleep effectively. Jackson then led him into his laboratory to show him his supply of ether. As Morton studied the colorless, sweet-smelling liquid, Jackson said, "This ether has been standing for some time." To work properly, he explained, the ether had to be highly refined and fresh.

Now Morton understood. His first batch of ether had been of high quality, but the second batch, which had come from another source, was apparently impure. Thinking he had just inspired Morton to try ether on patients, Jackson was pleased, too. He gave Morton a glass apparatus that he said was a better way to administer ether than pouring it on a handkerchief.

This meeting would lead to one of the greatest feuds in the history of science, but as Morton rushed from Jackson's laboratory, he felt elated. He headed to Burnett's, a chemical firm near his office, where he had bought the first batch of ether. Morton purchased a new bottle of the highest-quality ether Burnett's had, and carried the precious flask a short way to his old office.

Morton shut himself up in a room, sat down in his dental chair, and inhaled the ether, using Jackson's apparatus. It did not work well, so he resumed his old way of pouring it onto a handkerchief. Morton checked his watch, then breathed the ether until he was asleep.

He awoke to find that he had been unconscious between seven and eight minutes. He tried to stand but was so groggy that he fell back into his chair. Gradually his mind cleared and he regained the use of his limbs. Morton then ran into his workshop and began dancing about, shouting "Eureka! Eureka!" to his assistants and Dr. Hayden. He described what had happened and asked Hayden to meet him back at his office after supper so that they could discuss etherization. William Morton then headed home to Etherton in so joyous a mood that Elizabeth remembered it clearly many years later:

> That night he came home late, in a great state of excitement, but so happy that he could scarcely calm himself to tell me what had occurred; and I, too, became so excited that I could scarcely wait to hear. At last he told me of the

experiment upon himself, and I grew sick at heart as the thought came to me that he might have died there alone. He went on to say that he was resolved not to sleep that night until he had repeated the experiment, and declared that, late as it was, he must still find a patient.

After supper Morton returned to Boston, where he rejoined Dr. Hayden. The two dentists planned designs for ether inhalers, and discussed the possibility of etherizing patients. Their opportunity came sooner than they expected.

At a few minutes before nine that night, the office bell rang. In his doorway Morton found a man with bandages wrapped around his jaw. "Doctor, I've got the most frightful toothache," said the man, a music teacher named Eben Frost. Once in the office, Frost suddenly lost his courage. "My mouth is so sore I am afraid to have the tooth drawn," he told Dr. Morton. "Can't you mesmerize [hypnotize] me?"

"I can do something better," Morton answered. He sat Frost in the dental chair and convinced him that breathing a certain preparation would let him sleep through the tooth pulling. As Grenville Hayden held an oil lamp nearby to provide light, Morton saturated a handkerchief with ether and placed it over Frost's face. "Breathe deeply," Morton told Frost. The music teacher lost consciousness almost immediately.

William Morton had already made two serious mistakes. First, ether is highly flammable, so having Dr. Hayden hold the oil lamp near the patient's head could have caused a fire or explosion. Luckily, the ether did not ignite as Morton grabbed the tooth, twisted, then yanked it out. Morton and Hayden were congratulating each other when they realized that Frost wasn't awakening. Morton's second mistake was that he had covered Frost's nose and mouth with the handkerchief. A patient needs air with the ether to breathe properly. Fortunately, Frost had received enough air through the handkerchief to survive. Morton splashed a glass of water on

Frost's face, and the music teacher opened his eyes, looking around in bewilderment.

"Are you ready to have the tooth out?" Morton asked.

"I am ready," Eben Frost bravely answered.

"Well, it is out!" said Morton, pointing to the tooth on the floor.

"No!" Frost cried. "Glory! Hallelujah!"

Remembering what had happened to Horace Wells at his demonstration, Morton decided to take every precaution to back up his claims for ether. He handed Frost pen and paper and had him write out a certificate:

> This is to certify that I applied to Doctor Morton, at 9 o'clock this evening [September 30, 1846], suffering under the most violent toothache; that Doctor Morton took out his pocket-handkerchief, saturated it with a preparation of his, from which I breathed for about half a minute, and then was lost in sleep. In an instant I awoke, and saw my tooth lying on the floor. I did not experience the slightest pain whatever. I remained twenty minutes in his office afterward, and felt no unpleasant effects from the operation.
>
> Eben H. Frost,
> 42 Prince Street, Boston

Morton was careful to have Frost call the substance "a preparation" rather than "ether." Like Horace Wells, Morton wanted to help the world with his discovery. But unlike Wells, who said that laughing gas "should be as free as the air we breathe," Morton hoped to make a fortune from ether. He was worried that he wouldn't be able to patent his discovery if people learned that it was simply ether, so he decided to keep the nature of his anesthetic secret. Later that same night, Morton visited a writer for the *Boston Daily Journal*. He withheld the nature of his anesthetic from him, too, as shown by the next day's article:

Last evening, as we were informed by a gentleman who witnessed the operation, an ulcerated tooth was extracted from the mouth of an individual, without giving him the slightest pain. He was put into a kind of sleep, by inhaling a preparation, the effects of which lasted about three-quarters of a minute, just long enough to extract the tooth.

As Morton had hoped, Bostonians who read this article came to him to have teeth painlessly extracted. Over the next few days he had at least four or five opportunities to use ether, although he didn't call it that. He called his preparation Letheon, after Lethe, a river in Greek mythology from which dead souls drank in order to forget their earthly troubles.

Within a week of the Eben Frost operation, Morton felt ready to present his discovery to the world. On October 4 or 5 he visited Dr. John Collins Warren—whose harsh attitude had nearly destroyed Horace Wells almost two years earlier, but who now seemed more receptive to the possibility of anesthesia. Warren promised to inform Morton of the first opportunity to administer Letheon, which the famous surgeon knew by its smell contained ether.

On October 13, 1846, a young printer named Gilbert Abbott was brought into the Massachusetts General Hospital operating room. Dr. Warren was about to begin cutting a growth from beneath Gilbert's jaw when he remembered something. "I have promised Mr. Morton an opportunity to try a new remedy for preventing pain," Dr. Warren told Abbott. Would he be willing to try the method? Standing there with a knife in his hand, Warren made this an easy question to answer. The printer happily agreed.

So as to be near Massachusetts General Hospital, Morton and his family were temporarily living in Boston with a friend, Dr. Augustus Gould. On October 14, a note from the hospital was delivered to William Morton at Dr. Gould's home:

Dear Sir,

    *I write at the request of Dr. John Collins Warren
to invite you to be present Friday morning, October
16, at ten o'clock at the hospital to administer to a
patient who is then to be operated upon, the preparation you have invented to diminish the sensibility
to pain.*

His method of administering ether was Morton's greatest
concern. The handkerchief technique didn't allow him to control the amount and flow of the ether, nor was he satisfied with
Jackson's glass apparatus. Morton spent the two days before
the operation designing an inhaler with the help of his wife
and Dr. Gould. The three of them made sketch after sketch,
trying to create the safest and most effective method of deliv-

An exact replica of Dr. Morton's inhaler

ering ether to the patient. Finally, Morton took their design to the shop of an instrument maker named Chamberlain, who agreed to make the device.

William and Elizabeth hardly slept the night before the demonstration. Elizabeth had information that she was apparently keeping from her husband so as not to shake his confidence. Prominent doctors had visited her, advising that she talk her husband out of anesthetizing Gilbert Abbott. "I was told that one of two things was sure to happen," Elizabeth later wrote. "Either the test would fail and my husband would be ruined by the world's ridicule, or he would kill the patient and be tried for manslaughter." As for William Morton, ideas for slight improvements on the inhaler kept floating through his mind on that night before the operation.

Morton awoke at daybreak and was soon on his way to fetch Eben Frost, who had become a kind of dental mascot of his. No doubt by paying him, Morton always had Frost present whenever he used ether, to reassure his patients that the method was safe. By eight o'clock, Morton and Frost were at Chamberlain's shop. Morton hoped the last-second improvements on the inhaler would take just a few minutes, but the clock struck nine, then nine-thirty, and still the instrument maker was not done. As ten o'clock neared, William Morton went into a frenzy. Each passing minute was a fresh torture as he saw the great opportunity of his life disappearing.

Finally, at a few minutes after ten, Chamberlain handed him the device, which basically was a tube attached to a glass globe in which an ether-soaked sponge would be placed. Morton was a ludicrous sight as he dashed through the Boston streets with what looked like a goldfish bowl clutched to his chest and Eben Frost tagging behind. But Morton's face had a look of panic, for he knew that at any second the operation might proceed without him.

Meanwhile, the scene was solemn inside the Massachusetts General Hospital fourth-floor operating theater, now known

The old operating theater at Massachusetts General Hospital, now known as the Ether Dome

as the Ether Dome. The theater was much like a lecture hall, with about one hundred seats overlooking the operating stage. That Friday morning the seats were filled, for news of the event had spread, and so besides the usual Harvard doctors and students a number of other interested people had arrived. They included Dr. Wellington, there in the hope of seeing his former science student succeed in his demonstration.

Intensely angry to be kept waiting by the dentist, Dr.

Warren stood on the stage talking to the staff doctors. Everyone kept glancing at the doorways for a sign of Morton, but all that met their eyes was the Egyptian mummy standing against the wall to give the place a "scientific" look. The most anxious person of all was the young man strapped to the operating couch. A few minutes before, Gilbert Abbott had anticipated a painless operation. Now he saw that Dr. Warren was about to give up on Morton and begin the operation without him.

Finally, at 10:15, Dr. Warren told the audience in his most sarcastic tones, "As Dr. Morton has not arrived, I presume he is otherwise engaged." The spectators laughed, but then quieted as John Collins Warren picked up his knife and prepared to make the first incision.

Just then two breathless men rushed into the operating theater. Morton began to explain why he was late, but Warren cut him short. "Well, sir, your patient is ready," he said, pointing to Gilbert Abbott.

Morton explained to the audience that he was about to put the patient to sleep with Letheon. He had added oil of oranges and other aromatics to the ether in a not completely successful attempt to hide its telltale odor. Many in the audience knew by the smell that Letheon contained ether, even if they didn't realize that it was nothing but ether.

Once his apparatus was ready, Morton stepped up to the operating couch and clasped Gilbert Abbott's hand. "Here is a man who has breathed the preparation and can testify to its success," Morton told him. This was Eben Frost's cue to tell Abbott how his tooth had been pulled painlessly using Letheon. Finally, Morton asked Abbott, "Are you afraid?"

"No," the patient answered. "I feel confident, and will do precisely what you tell me."

Morton placed the tube leading from the glass globe into Abbott's mouth. The fumes from the ether-soaked sponge passed from the globe through the tube to Abbott's breathing

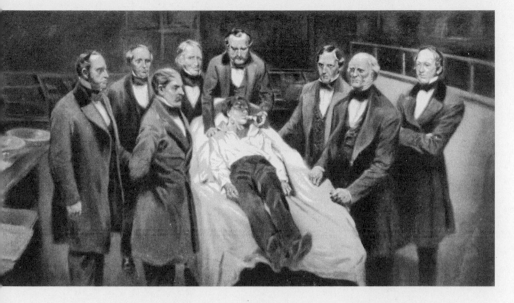

Dr. Morton (at patient's head) anesthetizing Gilbert Abbot;
as we view the scene, Dr. John Collins Warren is on
Morton's left.

passages and he soon nodded off. Morton looked closely at Abbott's face and felt his pulse to make certain that he was safely unconscious. Morton then displayed the fierce pride that had gotten him thrown out of Oxford Academy as a boy. Mocking the words of the country's greatest surgeon, he said, "*Your* patient is ready, doctor."

Elizabeth Morton, who was not at the operation but learned the details from witnesses, described what happened next:

> Then in all parts of the amphitheater there came a quick catching of the breath, followed by a silence almost death-like, as Dr. Warren stepped forward and prepared to operate.... The patient lay silent, with eyes closed as if in sleep; but everyone present fully expected to hear a shriek of agony ring out as the knife struck down into the sensitive

nerves. But the stroke came with no accompanying cry. Then another and another, and still the patient lay silent, sleeping, while the blood from severed arteries spurted forth. The surgeon was doing his work, and the patient was free from pain, so it seemed at least; and all in wonder strained their eyes and bent forward, following eagerly every step in the operation.

After cutting away the growth from under Gilbert Abbott's jaw, Dr. Warren sewed up and bandaged the wound. The audience continued to watch in silence, for something just as important as putting the patient to sleep had to occur for the procedure to be a success. Gilbert Abbott had to awaken. If he didn't, Morton would face a manslaughter charge and anesthesia probably would have to wait many more years to come into use.

Gilbert Abbott soon opened his eyes and looked around.

"Did you feel any pain?" Morton asked him.

"No," the patient answered.

Dr. Warren repeated Morton's question.

"I did not experience pain at any time," said Abbott, "though I knew that the operation was proceeding."

As Gilbert Abbott was carried away to recuperate, Dr. John Collins Warren faced the audience. "Gentlemen," he said quietly, "*this* is no humbug."

CHAPTER VI

"WE HAVE CONQUERED PAIN"

S oon after he put down his surgical knife, Dr. Warren picked up his pen and entered a report on the Gilbert Abbott operation in Massachusetts General Hospital's *Surgical Records 1846.* This huge volume still exists, along with the hospital's other old records dating back to its very first case in 1821, in a dimly lit vault deep beneath the Ether Dome. Dr. Warren's entry is still plainly readable:

> Before the operation began some time was lost in waiting for Dr. Morton, and ultimately it was thought he would not appear. At length he arrived and explained his detention by informing Dr. Warren that he had been occupied in preparing his apparatus, which consisted of a tube connected with a glass globe. This apparatus he then proceeded to apply, and after four or five minutes the patient appeared to be asleep, and the operation was performed, as herein described. To the surprise of Dr. Warren and the other gentlemen present, the patient did not shrink nor cry out.... After he had recovered his faculties, he said he had experi-

enced [no pain], but only a sensation like that of scraping the part with a blunt instrument, and he ever after continued to say he had not felt any pain....

As Warren wrote his report, William Morton was detained at the hospital by dozens of people who wanted to congratulate him. Finally, about twelve hours after he had left, Morton returned home in the late afternoon. He appeared so exhausted that for a moment Elizabeth was afraid the patient had died and her husband was about to be led off to jail. But he took her in his arms, and, with barely enough strength to talk, said, "Well, dear, I succeeded."

Unlike Crawford Long, Morton had plenty of people to publicize his achievement. Even as Morton held his wife in his arms, and as Dr. Warren set down his quill from *Surgical Records 1846*, news of the operation was going out to the rest of the world.

The first of many newspaper stories about the operation appeared the next day, October 17. Beneath the headline "Successful Operation" the *Boston Daily Journal* reported that "Dr. Morton, dentist, No. 19 Tremont Row...administered his preparations to produce sleep to a person about to undergo the operation of the extraction of a tumor from the neck." A New York City newspaper exclaimed, "It is the most glorious, nay, the most God-like discovery of this or any other age." Meanwhile, steamships carried the news to Europe, where the *People's Journal* of London proclaimed:

Hail, happy hour! that brings the glad tidings of another glorious victory. Oh, what delight for every feeling heart to find [that]...WE HAVE CONQUERED PAIN.... It is a victory not for today, not for our own time, but for another age, and all time—not for one nation, but for all nations, from generation to generation, as long as the world shall last.

THE PEOPLE'S JOURNAL. 25

times. One of the earliest pieces of education—of training—is to induce a babe to sleep regularly, and without the coaxing which consumes so much of the mother's time, and encourages so much waywardness on the part of the child. If a healthy child be early accustomed to a bed of its own, and if it is laid down at a sleepy moment, while the room is quiet, it will soon get into a habit of sleeping when laid down regularly, in warmth and stillness, after being well washed and satisfied with food. The process is natural; and it would happen easily enough if our ways did not interfere with nature. By a little care, a child may be attended to in the night without fully awakening it. By watching for its stirring, veiling the light, being silent and quick, the little creature may be on its pillow again without having quite waked up —to its own and its mother's great advantage.

Cleanliness is the removal of all that is unwholesome. Nature has made health dependent upon this, in the case of human beings of every age; and the more eminently, the younger they are. One great condition of an infant's welfare is the removal of all discharges whatever, by careful cleansing of the delicate skin in every crease and corner, every day; and of all clothing as soon as soiled. The perpetual washing of an infant's bibs, &c., is a great trouble to a busy mother; but less than to have the child ill from the smell of a sour pinafore, or from wet underclothes, or from a cap that holds the perspiration of a week's nights and days. It is a thing which must be done—the keeping all pure and sweet about the body of the little creature, that cannot help itself; and its look of welfare amply repays the trouble all the while.

Such are the offices to be rendered to the new-born infant. They consist in allowing Nature scope for her 'higher offices. By their faithful discharge, the human being is prepared to become in due season all that he is made capable of being —which may prove to be something higher than we are at present aware of.

THE PEOPLE'S SABBATH PRAYER.

From an Unpublished Lyric entitled " Life According to Law."

BY EBENEZER ELLIOTT.

Again, oh Lord! we humbly pray
   That thou wilt guide our steps aright:
Bless here, this day, tir'd labour's day!
   Oh, fill our souls with love and light!

For failing food, six days in seven
   We till the black town's dust and gloom;
But here we drink the breath of heav'n,
   And here to pray the poor have room.

The stately temple, built with hands,
   Throws wide its door to pomp and pride;
But in the porch their beadle stands,
   And thrusts the child of toil aside.

Therefore, we seek the daisied plain,
   Or climb the hills to touch thy feet;
Here, far from splendour's city fane,
   Thy weary sons and daughter meet.

Is it a crime to tell thee here,
   That here the sorely-tried are met,

To seek thy face, and find thee near,
   And on thy rock our feet to set?
Where, wheeling wide, the plover flies,
   Where sings the wood-lark on the tree,
Beneath the music of thy skies,
   Is it a crime to worship thee?

" We waited long, and sought thee, Lord,"
   Content to toil, but not to pine;
And with the weapons of thy word
   Alone, assail'd our foes and thine.
Thy truth and thee we bade them fear;
   They spurn thy truth and mock our groan!
"Thy counsels, Lord, they *will* not hear,
   And thou hast left them to their own."

THE GOOD NEWS FROM AMERICA.*

HAIL happy hour! that brings the glad tidings of another glorious victory. Oh, what delight for every feeling heart to find the new year ushered in with the announcement of this noble discovery of the power to still the sense of pain, and veil the eye and memory from all the horrors of an operation. And then to find it acted upon almost on the instant by our first operators, is as gratifying as unexpected. WE HAVE CONQUERED PAIN. This is indeed a glorious victory to announce; a victory of the pure intellect. And from America comes the happy news; from our brothers in another land, with whom we were lately going to war. Oh, shame be in the thought! This is indeed a glorious victory; but there is no blow struck, there has been no grappling together in the war of savage impulse, no bloodshed, no remorse. It is the victory of knowledge over ignorance, of good over evil: there is no alloy; all our finer sympathies are enlisted in one universal prayer of grateful rejoicing. Benevolence has its triumph. It is a victory not for to-day, nor for our own time, but for another age, and all time—not for one nation, but for all nations, from generation to generation, as long as the world shall last.

Yet, hark! there is no firing of cannon from the Tower—no banners waving in the air—no drums and fifes sounding before the conquering hero—no hubbub in the streets—no gazing multitudes thronging the towns to see the illuminations; no, these are for the most part but the instruments of war, the loud rejoicing of the passions of men triumphing over their fellow men. We have nothing to do with that now: but only to stretch forth our hand to soothe the agonising wounds the sword has caused, to allay the sufferings of the afflicted, to still the nerve and sense, whilst the knife performs its friendly office.

The rejoicing here is of the heart, in the smile, the tear of joy for suffering relieved, the still voice of the benevolent soul rejoicing inwardly; for to those who can grasp the full sense of the immense boon which has been given to us, it is, indeed, overpowering—the blessing is incalculable. Oh, let there be no exulting over those who have denied the possibility or the blessing of this good: let that pass. We poor despised mesmerisers have

* A practical paper on this most deeply interesting subject—Inhalation of Ether—will appear immediately in the *People's Journal.*

Yet while the news spread, for a few weeks the technique went no further than Massachusetts General Hospital because only one person was absolutely certain what was in Letheon and he wasn't ready to tell. William Morton hoped to become immensely wealthy by patenting Letheon and licensing doctors and dentists around the world to use it. Until he secured the patent, he planned to keep secret the fact that Letheon was ether plus some harmless substances to disguise the smell.

Soon after the Gilbert Abbott operation, Morton visited Richard Eddy, Boston commissioner of patents, who had good news for him. In Eddy's opinion, Morton could obtain a patent and make a fortune from Letheon. Apparently Eddy said that after a few more trials with Letheon at Massachusetts General Hospital, he would file the patent papers.

Before Letheon's introduction, Massachusetts General Hospital had averaged about one operation per week. Suddenly patients who had been avoiding surgery changed their minds. The day after the Gilbert Abbott operation, Morton administered Letheon to a woman who had a tumor removed from her arm. More operations followed. In his notes in *Surgical Records 1846* Dr. Warren wrote that within "a few days its [Letheon's] success was established, and its use resorted to in every considerable operation in the city of Boston."

Yet there were still many skeptics in the medical world. Morton had proven that Letheon allowed patients to sleep through rather big operations. But could it keep patients asleep through a "capital" (extremely serious) operation—the amputation of a limb, for example?

In early November Dr. John Warren asked Morton to administer Letheon in a capital case. The patient, twenty-one–year-old Alice Mohan, had entered the hospital in March with a diseased knee. Infection had set in, and her leg needed to be amputated. However, Alice's dread of the pain was so intense that she refused the surgery, preferring to die of infection in her hospital bed. Now that Letheon was available, she changed her mind, and her operation was scheduled for November 7, 1846.

William Morton, meanwhile, faced one of the most difficult decisions in medical history. In the minds of some doctors at Massachusetts General Hospital and many more doctors at other hospitals, he was rapidly turning into a villain rather than a hero. A cardinal rule of medicine is that discoveries must be shared. Each day that Morton kept Letheon's ingredients secret prolonged the agony of surgery for patients around the world. Morton felt guilty about this, but he also felt he had the right to make the world wait a little longer until his patent went through. Hadn't he sacrificed his dental practice to experiment with ether, and risked his reputation with the Gilbert Abbott operation?

The Massachusetts Medical Society had a specific rule against secret remedies, which Dr. Warren and the hospital's other surgeons broke each time they let Morton administer Letheon. As the day of Alice Mohan's operation neared, the cry for Morton to reveal the recipe for Letheon grew louder. At a special meeting in early November the Massachusetts Medical Society voted to forbid its members from participating in operations using Letheon until Morton revealed its contents.

Newspapers announced the time and place of Alice Mohan's surgery, so that on the morning of November 7, the operating theater was even more crowded than it had been for the Gilbert Abbott operation. Morton hoped that Dr. Warren and a few others who sympathized with his desire to patent Letheon before revealing its contents would convince the hospital staff to defy the society's order. While the doctors argued the issue, Morton waited in a small room. Finally, he was told of their final decision: Unless he had a last-second change of heart, Alice Mohan's leg would be cut off without the use of Letheon. Morton immediately went to the room where the doctors were meeting. Probably with as much relief as regret, he revealed his secret: Letheon was nothing but ether and some agents to disguise the smell.

Alice Mohan was on the operating couch when William Morton entered the theater. As Morton prepared his inhaler, Dr. George Hayward, the young woman's surgeon, told the huge audience, "The patient, Alice Mohan, will inhale a vapor to allay the pain of the operation. The fluid whose vapor will be used is sulfuric ether." Dr. Warren explained why the amputation was necessary, then Morton spoke a few reassuring words to Alice and placed the inhaler in her mouth. She was just starting to complain about the ether's smell when she drifted off to sleep. Dr. Hayward pulled a pin from beneath his frock coat lapel and jabbed Alice in the arm, with no reaction. Satisfied that she was deeply asleep, Hayward picked up his surgical knife and cut off her leg in 105 seconds.

Once he finished sewing her stitches, Dr. Hayward shook Alice's arm. "I guess you've been asleep, Alice," Hayward said.

"I think I have, sir," the awakening patient mumbled.

"We have brought you here for an amputation. Are you ready?"

"Yes, sir, I am ready."

Hayward then picked up the amputated leg from the floor and held it up for Alice to see. "It is all done!"

The excitement in the operating theater dwarfed what had occurred after the Gilbert Abbott operation. "Men were beside themselves with joy," wrote a physician from Atlanta, Georgia, who witnessed the operation. "They clapped their hands, stamped, and yelled."

When doctors throughout the world learned that they could put patients to sleep for capital operations with a substance obtainable at any chemist's, their reaction was much the same. Within a few days, William Morton was being called the greatest medical hero the country had ever produced and people were trying to outdo each other with praise for the breakthrough. It was called "the world's most important medical discovery" and "the greatest gift ever made to suffering

Dr. Oliver Wendell Holmes

humanity." Dr. John Collins Warren, casting aside his usual restraint, wrote, "It is the most valuable discovery ever made, because it frees suffering humanity from pain." Wanting the world to remember where the great advance took place, Warren added, "The student who from distant lands or in distant ages may visit this spot [Massachusetts General Hospital] will view it with increased interest, as he remembers that here was first demonstrated one of the most glorious truths of science."

People immediately began searching for a better name than Letheon. From old texts, Dr. Oliver Wendell Holmes learned that the Greek physician Dioscorides had coined the word *anesthesia,* meaning "without feeling," nearly eighteen hundred years earlier, and in a letter to Morton he advised that this word be resurrected:

> *November 21, 1846*
>
> *Dear Sir,*
>
> *Everybody wants to have a hand in a great discovery. All I do is to give you a hint or two as to names, or the names to be applied to the state produced and the agent. The state should, I think, be called Anesthesia. The adjective will be Anesthetic. Thus we might say the state of anesthesia, or the anesthetic state....*

Dr. Holmes's suggestions were adopted, and the process that was spreading through the medical world became known as anesthesia. The first surgery under anesthesia in England was performed on December 21, 1846—six weeks after the Alice Mohan operation. Dr. Robert Liston, the "quickest man with the knife in England," performed it in London on a patient with a diseased thigh. Liston then made the famous comment, "This Yankee dodge has mesmerism beaten all hollow!" (meaning that the American invention for avoiding pain was far better than hypnotism). To this day, anesthesia is occasionally referred to as the "Yankee dodge."

Ether was soon being used in France, Germany, and other nations. In Russia they called it "the greatest blessing, a gift from heaven." In Austria it was "the greatest discovery of our century." In Scotland, a family named a newborn baby Anesthesia.

And what of William Morton, who had introduced anesthesia to the world? He received praise in every written language in existence. Yet in the days after the Alice Mohan operation, his struggle was just beginning.

CHAPTER VII

WHOSE DISCOVERY IS IT?

Once William Morton revealed that Letheon was just ether, his hopes for making a fortune dimmed. Yet they did not disappear altogether, for there was also the inhaler that he had designed. When presented as a package, Commissioner Richard Eddy felt, Morton's etherization process still stood a good chance of being patented.

As Eddy prepared the patent papers for presentation to the government, Morton worked out a licensing plan. Dentists were to pay him between ten and several hundred dollars a year for the rights to etherization, depending on the size of the city where they practiced. Surgeons were to pay 25 percent of their fees from operations using ether. Had Morton actually received what he wanted, he would have become one of the richest people who ever lived.

Morton hoped to train and station agents around the country who would distribute his inhalers, see that the process was used safely, and make certain that the proper fees were paid. Three days after the Gilbert Abbott operation, Morton wrote to Horace Wells, who was then trying to sell his foot-pumped

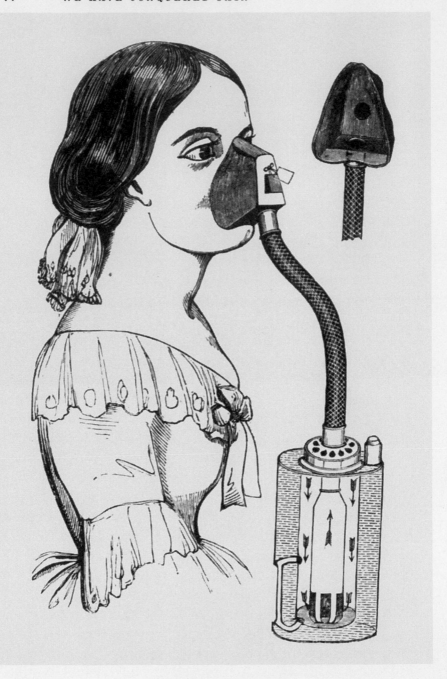

An early anesthesia inhaler

shower baths, asking him to be one of his agents:

> *Boston, October 19, 1846*
>
> *Friend Wells:*
>
> *Dear Sir:—I write to inform you that I have dis-
> covered a preparation by inhaling which a person is
> thrown into a sound sleep. The time required to pro-
> duce sleep is only a few moments, and the time in
> which persons remain asleep can be regulated at
> pleasure. While in this state the severest surgical or
> dental operations may be performed, the patient not
> experiencing the slightest pain. I have patented it,
> and am now about sending out agents to dispose of
> the right to use it.... My object in writing you is to
> know if you would not like to visit New York and
> the other cities to dispose of rights....*

Morton had actually just begun the patent process, and
although he asserted that he was "sending out agents," Wells
was probably the first person he approached. Within a week,
Horace Wells visited the Boston office that he had briefly shared
with Morton. Wells watched Morton administer Letheon to several patients, then extract their teeth as they slept.

Despite the method's success, Wells refused to become one
of Morton's agents. In keeping with his generous attitude that
nitrous oxide "should be as free as the air we breathe," Wells
felt that Morton's process shouldn't be patented or used to
make a profit. But Wells may have also been growing jealous
of his former student. When he returned from Morton's office,
Elizabeth asked him, "Has Morton discovered anything new?"

"No!" Horace Wells told his wife. "It is my old discovery!"

Back in Hartford, Wells followed Morton's meteoric rise to
fame. As he read about the subsequent operations at
Massachusetts General Hospital, climaxing with the Alice
Mohan surgery, Wells began to think that all this praise and

fame could have been his had he held the gasbag to the patient's nose just a few seconds longer. The more he thought about it, the more Wells felt that he wasn't receiving his fair share of the credit. Hadn't he successfully given patients laughing gas more than a year before Morton began administering ether? Hadn't he blazed the trail for Morton with the Boston doctors, even taking him along at his unsuccessful demonstration in early 1845?

In December of 1846 Wells summoned the courage to begin campaigning on his own behalf. He started with a letter that appeared December 9 in the *Hartford Courant*. Wells recounted how he had seen people endure "severe blows" after breathing laughing gas, and how this led him to the December 11, 1844, experiment in which Dr. Riggs removed his wisdom tooth. "I then performed the same operation on twelve or fifteen others with the same results," Wells continued. He then related the most painful episode of his professional life, blaming himself that "the gas bag was by mistake withdrawn much too soon," yet asserting that the patient experienced "some pain, but not as much as usually attends the operation." He closed by saying: "After making the above statement of facts, I leave it for the public to decide to whom belongs the honor of this discovery."

The day after this letter appeared, Wells wrote to Morton, deriding his accomplishments as "nothing more than what I can prove priority of discovery by at least 18 months…. Now, I do not wish, or expect, to make any money out of this invention, nor to cause you to be the loser; but I have resolved to give a history of its introduction, that I may have what credit belongs to me."

Despite writing these letters, Horace Wells had not overcome his impulse to flee trouble. He had hatched a new scheme to purchase paintings in Paris which he would resell in the United States. By the time Morton could respond to his letter, Wells was aboard a ship bound for France.

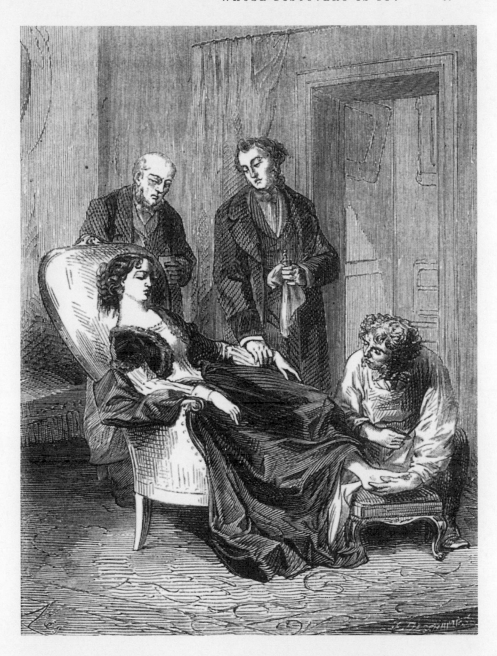

The use of anesthetics was dangerous in the early days when doctors didn't know the proper dosages to administer; this young woman died from an anesthetic overdose in 1848.

William Morton had another foe who wouldn't go away as easily. A few days after the Gilbert Abbott operation, Dr. Charles Jackson visited Morton. Jackson had learned from his close friend Commissioner Eddy that Morton was applying for a patent for etherization.

"You stand to make a good deal by it," Jackson told Morton. "I believe I must make a professional charge for my advice," he said, referring to his information about the ether toothache drops and the necessity of using ether that was pure.

"Why in this case, more than in any other?" asked Morton, who had questioned his old medical tutor on many matters over the years without paying for the answers.

Jackson had anticipated the question. "The advice has been useful to you," he insisted. "You should make a good deal out of the patent, and ought to make me a compensation." Jackson said the fee he had in mind was five hundred dollars—quite a sum in those days.

Morton did not want to anger Jackson, who was an influential man in scientific circles. He was also relieved that Jackson seemed to want only money rather than credit for the discovery. "I will pay you five hundred dollars—if ten percent of the profits on my patent amount to that," Morton told him. Pleased at having taken the first step toward claiming a part of the discovery, Jackson agreed to this and departed.

Jackson has long been portrayed as the villain in the anesthesia controversy. But if his life is examined, his motives for claiming other people's discoveries become somewhat understandable.

Charles Thomas Jackson was born into a prominent and wealthy family in Plymouth, Massachusetts, on June 21, 1805. He was a descendant of the early settlers of Plymouth, founded by the Pilgrims as New England's first town. When Charles was eight, his family moved into a huge mansion overlooking Plymouth Harbor. Only about three hundred feet away from

Charles Jackson's childhood home in Plymouth, Massachusetts

the east parlor window was Plymouth Rock, which the Pilgrims reportedly stepped on when they landed in 1620.

Charles Jackson received the best education the country could offer. He attended a private school in nearby Duxbury, and then was tutored in medicine by Walter Channing, a famous physician. In 1825 Jackson entered Harvard Medical School, where Channing was the dean. Jackson's interests branched out to geology and chemistry while he was at Harvard. He began publishing geological papers in scientific journals in 1828, when he was twenty-three. He graduated the next year, and won the university's prestigious Boylston Prize for his paper on the disease diabetes.

Harvard was America's oldest and most respected college, yet there were European universities with even greater reputations. Within weeks of his graduation from medical school, Jackson sailed for France. He continued his medical education at the University of Paris, while also studying with some of the world's leading geologists. Jackson became especially friendly with Elie de Beaumont, a French geologist who advanced our knowledge on mountain formation.

Jackson studied in Paris for over a year, then set out on a walking tour of Europe. In Austria, he performed autopsies on two hundred patients who had died of the disease cholera, later publishing his findings in the *New England Journal of Medicine*. In Italy, he visited Vesuvius, an active volcano. Before returning to America, Jackson stopped again in Paris, where he bought a recently invented device called an electromagnet for performing electrical experiments. Soon after, in October 1832, Jackson sailed from Le Havre, France, aboard the *Sully*.

It happened that the famous portrait painter Samuel F. B. Morse was one of Jackson's fellow passengers. The two spent much time together during the six-week ocean crossing. Morse had long been interested in electricity, and was fascinated when Jackson showed him how his electromagnet worked. Morse was especially intrigued by Jackson's theory that the apparatus could be used to send messages over long distances.

Upon his return home, Jackson opened a medical practice in Boston. Soon after, in 1834, he married Bostonian Susan Bridge, with whom he would have six daughters and four sons. Charles and Susan Jackson became friends with some famous people, including poet Henry Wadsworth Longfellow and essayist Ralph Waldo Emerson, whom Jackson's older sister, Lydia, married in 1835. For a time Jackson also remained close with Samuel Morse, who painted the best portrait we have of Jackson as a young man.

Charles Jackson continued to accept private medical students, including William Morton, but he did not practice medicine for long. Some claimed he left medicine because his

This portrait of Charles T. Jackson was painted by Samuel F. B. Morse while the two men were still friends.

arrogant manner annoyed his patients. Yet Jackson could be charming when he chose, so a poor bedside manner was probably not the reason. It seems more likely that Jackson had too many interests to settle down to the workaday life of a doctor. When he began receiving offers for his geological services, he accepted. He became state geologist of Maine in 1836, and of Rhode Island and New Hampshire in 1839. This allowed him the travel he loved, and provided opportunity for studying minerals, plants, animals, and other natural wonders in a variety of places.

Jackson visited much of the country during his long career

as a geologist. In fact, few people of the 1800s saw as much of the United States as Charles T. Jackson. He was inexhaustible in his pursuit of knowledge. He dove to the bottom of a New Hampshire pond for a sample of mud that he suspected contained iron ore. He climbed giant sequoia trees in California to measure their size. When he wasn't traveling, he wrote, producing 450 scientific articles in his lifetime. Dozens of his essays were about gold, copper, and coal deposits he had investigated, but he also wrote on such varied topics as mastodon bones, meteorites, and the value of eating raisins for energy while on expeditions.

Jackson knew so much about so many subjects that he was widely regarded as a genius. He was not a happy genius, however. Growing up a stone's throw from Plymouth Rock, attending the country's oldest college, meeting the famous scientists of France, seeing his sister marry Ralph Waldo Emerson—all of these events planted a yearning in Jackson to make a great scientific discovery. This goal always seemed to be just out of reach for Jackson, but not for people he considered less worthy than himself.

The first time his obsession got the best of him involved one of the most famous cases in the history of medicine. William Beaumont, a doctor in Michigan, had saved the life of Alexis St. Martin, a fur trapper shot in the stomach. St. Martin was left with a permanent opening or "window" into his stomach through which Dr. Beaumont studied digestion, greatly increasing our understanding of the process. During a visit to Boston in 1834, Beaumont gave Jackson a sample of digestive juice for analysis. It irked Jackson that a prominent chemist like himself should miss out on studying St. Martin, while Beaumont just happened to be in the right place when the unusual patient came along. Implying that he was the main scientist in the digestive studies, Jackson petitioned the United States government to order that St. Martin remain with him in Boston. The petition went all the way to the United States secretary of war, but was turned down.

What happened with Samuel Morse vexed Jackson far more. Inspired by Jackson's talks aboard the *Sully,* Morse turned from art to science. For five years he worked on an electrical device that would send messages over long distances. Morse finally succeeded in 1837 with the creation of his electromagnetic telegraph. As Morse's fame grew, Jackson sought more credit than just being his inspiration. Although he had done no work to develop the telegraph, Jackson began to proclaim himself as the brains behind the invention and Morse as the workman who carried out his ideas. When Morse refused to acknowledge him as co-inventor, Jackson befriended newspaper editors and arranged for them to print favorable stories about him, including this article that appeared in the *Boston Post* in the spring of 1839:

> We are informed that the invention of the electro-magnetic telegraph, which has been claimed by Mr. S. F. B. Morse of New York, is entirely due to our fellow citizen, Dr. Charles T. Jackson, who first conceived the idea of such an instrument during his return voyage from Europe on the packet ship *Sully* in October 1832.

Jackson worked for many years for credit for the telegraph. He failed, as he did in a third attempt to steal another person's discovery. This battle was over the invention of the explosive called guncotton, which Jackson insisted should be credited to him rather than to the German chemist Christian Schönbein.

When he came to live with the Jacksons in 1844, William Morton viewed Jackson as having everything he dreamed about. Jackson was an M.D., widely published, respected as far away as Europe, and wealthy, owning not only the Beacon Hill home in Boston but also the family mansion in Plymouth. Morton knew that Jackson had been rebuffed in regard to the telegraph, but he had no clue as to just how frustrated the scientist was. At this time perhaps only Samuel Morse, who referred to Jackson as "a lunatic," realized that the man was becoming deranged over his desire for greatness.

Family tragedies added to Jackson's turmoil during this period. In 1841 his daughter, Susan Frances, died at the age of a year and eleven months. In 1849 his son Henry died at the age of only seven months.

While Morton idolized Jackson, the famous scientist viewed the young dentist with growing irritation. The way Morton used him to boost his own career reminded Jackson of the Samuel Morse episode. First there was the certificate for the gold dental solder that Morton had requested. Then there were the toothache drops that put Morton on the ether trail. Jackson let off some steam when he exploded at Morton for being late to Sunday dinner. Yet even after leaving Jackson's home, Morton continued to pick his brain, he felt. Hadn't Jackson's information that the ether must be highly refined and fresh enabled Morton to achieve fame with the Gilbert Abbott operation?

For a few days after that operation, Jackson watched from the shadows as everyone heaped praise on Morton. Jackson waited for Morton to mention his role in the breakthrough, but not so much as a thank you came from the dentist. Jackson also learned from his friend Commissioner Eddy that Morton was trying to patent the discovery with no mention of Charles T. Jackson, either. Jackson told Eddy that he deserved a share of the patent for his advice, and was so convincing that the Boston commissioner of patents began to take his side. Then, on October 23, 1846, Jackson visited Morton to request the fee for his advice.

Morton agreed to the five hundred dollars, but Jackson hadn't come just for the money. He still hoped that Morton would thank him and tell the world that he had taken part in the discovery. As before, Morton did not acknowledge that Jackson's information had been of help to him.

Two weeks later, when the world applauded Morton for revealing that Letheon was simply ether, Jackson's wounded

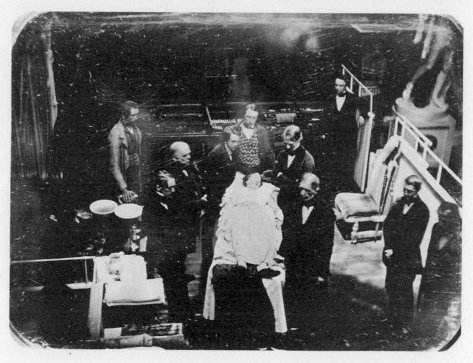

An 1848 surgical operation performed using ether

feelings turned to bitter hatred. His information had been *the* key to Morton's success, Jackson realized. He berated himself for asking only five hundred dollars from Morton, and told Eddy that he not only deserved his name on the patent but also 10 percent of the profits. Jackson broadcast this around Boston, confiding in Dr. Warren that "I was the person who suggested the use of ether to Morton."

Eddy felt that Morton should avoid a fight and agree to Jackson's new demands. Besides, Eddy told Morton, "The patent will have the benefit of Dr. Jackson's name and skill." To keep the peace, Morton followed Eddy's advice, while still maintaining that Jackson didn't really deserve any credit or money. On November 12, 1846, just eight days after Patent Number 4836 was granted to Horace Wells for his shower bath, Patent Number 4848 for ether anesthesia was granted jointly to William Morton and Charles Jackson. It was strictly a business deal, for Morton now despised Jackson nearly as much as Jackson loathed him.

Yet even having his name on the patent and being guaranteed 10 percent of the profits did not satisfy Jackson for long. He became convinced that he deserved most of the credit and reward, and that Morton had been merely his tool in carrying out his ideas. Jackson began telling everyone in Boston who would listen that the dentist had been his "servant" at Massachusetts General Hospital.

Three days after the patent went through, Richard Eddy visited Jackson to see why he was still so upset. Eddy found his friend in a highly agitated state. "I claim the whole of it, it is mine!" Jackson kept repeating. "Morton did nothing but under my prescription!" Later that evening Jackson burst into Dr. Gould's house, where the Mortons were still living, and where Morton was at that moment discussing Jackson's continuing anger with Gould and Eddy. "I can prove it, I advised Morton to use ether at the Massachusetts General Hospital!" Jackson raved.

For the first time, William Morton realized that Jackson was becoming demented over the issue. Eddy managed to calm Jackson so that Morton could explain that Jackson's name on the patent was proof of how invaluable his advice had been. But Morton also insisted that most of the proceeds should be his, since he would have been the one to suffer had the Gilbert Abbott operation failed. This quieted Jackson, who seemed content to have some of the credit—at least for the time being. Jackson regained his composure, and there is no record of any more such outbursts from him until a summer day twenty-seven years later. However, if William Morton thought his troubles with Jackson were ended, he was sadly mistaken, for the famous scientist was about to reverse their roles in the controversy.

CHAPTER VIII

THE BATTLE TO THE DEATH, PART I

Charles Jackson's brother-in-law Ralph Waldo Emerson coined many sayings, two of which are fitting for the story of anesthesia: "Invention breeds invention" and "The reward of a thing well done is to have done it." The people involved in the development of anesthesia built on each other's work so much that it became difficult to determine whom to credit for the discovery. In the end, about all that any of them received was the honor of helping humanity.

After his tantrum, Jackson realized that anger had fogged his mind. It wasn't the money he wanted, for he had plenty of that. What he sought was credit for the discovery. He had two advantages in the battle with Morton, and with Wells, who had just begun asserting his claims before sailing for France. First, Jackson had powerful scientific friends in Europe, whose opinions, if shaped properly, might tip the decision in his favor. Second, Morton and Wells had both abandoned dentistry for the time being and needed money. The longer Jackson delayed the verdict as to who had discovered anesthesia, the more Morton and Wells could be made to look like money-hungry opportunists. Meanwhile, Charles T. Jackson would appear to be interested only in helping humanity through his discovery and in receiving the credit he deserved.

Jackson wrote letters to famous European scientists, crediting himself with the discovery. He began with Elie de Beaumont, whom he had befriended in France nearly twenty years earlier, and who belonged to the French Academy of Sciences, the world's leading scientific organization of the time.

"[I wish] to communicate through you to the Academy a discovery I have made," Jackson wrote in French. "I induced a dentist of this city to administer the vapors of ether to persons from whom he was to extract teeth. I then had him go to the Massachusetts General Hospital and administer ether to a patient about to undergo a painful operation."

On January 18, 1847, the French Academy of Sciences met to discuss the great American discovery. The members began to praise William Morton when Elie de Beaumont interrupted to read Jackson's letter. Jackson's claims pleased the French scientists, for Jackson had studied in France under several of them. The scientists left their meeting impressed with Jackson's fair-sounding suggestion: "I should be deeply grateful if the Academy would have the goodness to appoint a commission to prove the correctness of my assertions." Why would he want them to investigate his claims if they were not true?

Jackson wrote similar letters to the German scientist Baron Alexander von Humboldt and to other great scientists around the world. So believable were Jackson's claims that people in Austria called the process "Jacksonizing" instead of anesthesia.

William Morton was thunderstruck when the February mail from Europe reached Boston and he read about Jackson's success at the Paris meeting. He realized now that allowing Jackson's name on the patent along with his own had been a terrible blunder. He had thought of it as a bit of thanks to Jackson, and a way to appease him. But it could just as easily be interpreted in the opposite way—that Jackson was the main discoverer and was just humoring Morton.

The only ways for Morton to present his case to the European scientists were in person or in writing. Morton didn't want to leave the country, for Jackson would surely undermine him at home during his absence. This left writing, but Morton was worried about that, too. If it came to his word against Jackson's, who would the European scientists believe?

One day in late February, William Morton stormed over to Jackson's Beacon Hill laboratory and accused Jackson of plotting against him to steal his discovery. The tables were turned now, for it was Morton who raved and Jackson who listened calmly. When Morton threatened a lawsuit, Jackson explained that it had all been a misunderstanding. His letter had given Morton proper credit, but Elie de Beaumont, as his friend, had overemphasized Jackson's role in the discovery. He would fix everything, Jackson promised. He would see to it that a newspaper article was published explaining that it had been a joint discovery, and send copies of it on the Boston mail boat that was due to sail to Europe on the first of March.

Jackson's explanation made sense, and pacified Morton. He even felt a little sheepish for accusing Jackson of being a thief. Yes, he could see that it had all been a mistake, said Morton, pleased that Jackson himself would correct it in writing.

Over the next few days, Jackson executed a devilish plan. He convinced Edward Everett, president of the American Academy of Arts and Sciences in Boston (and president of Harvard University), to let him read a paper to the academy on March 2 explaining his side of the controversy. Jackson then visited the editor of the Boston *Daily Advertiser* and offered him an exclusive story about the ether discovery, including the speech he planned to make to the American Academy. The grateful editor leaped at the chance to publish Jackson's story.

Jackson wanted to make it seem like the American Academy had hailed him as the discoverer after hearing his speech, but there was a problem. The newspaper article was to come out March 1—the day before the speech. Having often distorted past events, Jackson now arranged the future to his liking as well. His *Daily Advertiser* article made it seem as if his speech had already been made and the academy had acknowledged him as the discoverer of ether anesthesia.

As March 1 neared, Morton grew anxious about the article that Jackson had promised to write. He paid Jackson another angry visit on Sunday, February 28. The mail boat was sailing the next day. Why was there no article yet? Again, Jackson soothed him. "I have prepared an article to appear in the *Daily Advertiser* tomorrow morning," he said, promising to rush copies of the newspaper to the mail boat before it sailed.

Still suspicious, Morton asked, "May I see a copy?"

"My copy is already at the printer's," Jackson answered.

Jackson kept his word—in one way. The *Daily Advertiser* article appeared the next morning, and Jackson loaded hundreds of copies onto the mail boat before its departure. But when Morton read the article, he was crushed to find that there was nothing in it about him at all. He was also astonished to learn about Jackson's great success at an American Academy meeting that hadn't yet taken place.

Now not only William Morton, but also Edward Everett, Dr. John Warren, and many other people were outraged. Jackson never did make his speech to the academy on March 2, but instead was reprimanded by Boston's leading scientists. Still, as the *Daily Advertiser* was passed around and reprinted in Europe, the damage was done. Here was proof that Jackson was the discoverer, claimed Elie de Beaumont and others who saw the article. And since Morton, trusting Jackson, had submitted nothing in his own behalf, the Europeans became even more convinced that the dentist couldn't be the originator of ether anesthesia.

Also in 1847, Drs. Warren and Hayward wrote essays and petitions naming Morton as the discoverer. Realizing that not offering the world a description of his work had been another grave mistake, Morton went into a writing frenzy to correct this. In September of 1847 he published a booklet in Boston about the discovery, and followed it with a pamphlet called *Memoir on Sulfuric Ether,* printed in Paris, France, that November. When they read *Morton's Memoir,* as it became known, the scientists in Europe were thrown into confusion. Now they didn't know whom to believe, Jackson or Morton.

Morton's Memoir did a wonderful job of presenting his case. He showed no animosity toward his enemy, and even related how Jackson had been of invaluable assistance. But, Morton added, "All that he communicated to me I could have got from other well informed chemists, or from some books." Morton closed his argument by saying that he had been the one who "risked reputation, and sacrificed time and money." *Morton's Memoir* ended with the sad words, "I believe I am the only person in the world to whom this discovery has, so far, been a pecuniary [monetary] loss."

Morton actually *was* losing money from the discovery. He hired a staff to license his etherization process around the country, ordered thousands of inhalers manufactured in anticipation of quickly selling them, but never even regained his initial investment. The first bad omen came during the war the United States fought with Mexico between 1846 and 1848. Morton's offer to sell his inhalers to the United States Army at discount prices and to instruct its surgeons in the process was refused. The army went ahead and etherized patients using its own inhalers without paying Morton one cent.

Seeing that the government that had granted Morton the patent for etherization would not pay him, surgeons and dentists around the country wondered why *they* should do so. After all, ether could be obtained from any chemist. As for Morton's inhaler, it wasn't much more than a jar with a rubber tube sticking out of it, which any instrument maker could create. Many of those who had already ordered Morton's inhalers sent back the devices, demanding refunds. William Morton, who had returned with his family to Etherton and had resumed his dental practice, was sinking into debt.

Jackson did his best to intensify his enemy's financial woes. On May 26, 1847, Jackson sent a friend to Morton's Boston office. Ripping up the business agreement between Jackson and Morton, the friend indignantly said, "Dr. Jackson does not want the ten percent of the profits which he had bargained for. He feels it would just burn in his pockets as so much blood money."

That night Jackson attended the yearly Massachusetts Medical Society dinner, where he was one of the speakers. "Honored colleagues, as the discoverer of anesthesia...," he began. Jackson discussed "his" discovery, then explained that he had been fooled into placing his name on the patent. "I was not told," he said, "that the purpose of the patent was to make profit out of the sufferings of mankind." He finished by saying that, unlike a certain Boston dentist, he was now presenting ether anesthesia as a free gift to the world.

Part of the audience realized that Jackson was giving away something that wasn't profitable and that wasn't his. The famed geologist Louis Agassiz rose and said, "If Dr. Morton had killed the first patient to whom he gave ether, would you have accepted the blame as you are now claiming the credit?" To this, Jackson had no answer. Still, despite the fact that Boston was the town most solidly in Morton's corner, many in the audience applauded Jackson's generosity. Morton's efforts to keep Letheon's ingredients secret and to make a fortune from it seemed utterly selfish by comparison.

Jackson had even more fiendish schemes to ruin Morton. By the spring of 1847, Morton had spent so much money on his inhalers that, even though he had returned to dentistry, he was forced to borrow large sums from several Bostonians. Jackson learned who the lenders were and warned them to demand their money back, convincing them that Morton couldn't escape debt now that the patent was proving unprofitable.

Two evenings after the Massachusetts Medical Society dinner, Morton came home to Etherton to find a stranger pacing back and forth on the veranda. "As head of this household I demand to know your business," Morton said. The stranger explained that he was the bailiff, a messenger from the sheriff. A man who had lent Morton money wanted it repaid. If Morton couldn't do this soon, the bailiff had orders to seize all his belongings.

Incredibly, Jackson even managed to wreck Morton's dental practice. Today most doctors and dentists request payment at the time of service. But in the 1800s demanding payment was considered unprofessional, and patients commonly took weeks or months to pay their bills. Somehow Jackson obtained a list of the patients who owed Morton money. He arranged for legal papers to be served on them, demanding immediate payment of their bills, and made it appear that Dr. Morton had taken this action.

The morning after the bailiff's visit, Dr. Morton was greeted by angry patients at his office door. How dare he serve legal papers on them! Didn't he think they would pay their bills? Well, there were other dentists in Boston! All day they streamed in to berate him. Morton explained that he hadn't served the papers, yet he lost many patients all the same.

Morton managed to prevent the sheriff from seizing his property, but he had to take out still more loans to pay those lenders who demanded their money. With his patients disappearing, his chances of ever escaping debt seemed remote.

As William Morton's problems grew, Horace Wells's fortunes were on the upswing. He felt pleased about asserting his cause in the *Hartford Courant* before his trip to France, and found the voyage relaxing. After three and a half weeks at sea, he reached France around February 1, 1847. Perhaps in the back of his mind Wells realized that he could accomplish more in Paris than buying paintings. It soon became clear that he had come to the perfect place at the ideal time to win support in the anesthesia controversy.

Paris was still buzzing over Elie de Beaumont's presentation of Jackson's letter to the French Academy of Sciences about two weeks earlier. Thanks to this letter, French opinion had swung from Morton's to Jackson's favor. But Horace Wells had the advantage of being there in person, and his claims that he had succeeded with nitrous oxide prior to the Morton-Jackson triumphs seemed believable. Dr. Christopher Brewster, an American dentist living in Paris, befriended Wells and arranged for him to speak before scientific societies, where Horace's modesty and sweet, gentle spirit won over many of his listeners. Wells admitted that his failure at Massachusetts General Hospital had been his own fault for removing the gasbag too soon. He felt no grudge against Morton and Jackson, who deserved praise for their work. But the simple fact was that he, Horace Wells, had been first.

For a few days Wells moved into the first spot in France. He was honored with balls and dinners, presented with a carriage said to be second in elegance only to that of King Louis Philippe, and reportedly was asked to remain in France as the king's dentist. Wells basked in his momentary glory, but people soon realized that he hadn't offered proof of his statements. Wells must return home and write up his claims, the French scientists told him, which they would then evaluate.

Invigorated by a new purpose in life, Wells began writing while still in Europe. In the February 17, 1847, edition of a journal called *Galignani's Messenger,* he published a long letter claiming the discovery. Ten days later Wells left Paris, and on March 4 he sailed for Boston from Liverpool, England. He must have spent all his time aboard the *Hibernia* writing, for on March 30, only a day or two after arriving in Hartford, he published *History of the Discovery of the Application of Nitrous Oxide Gas, Ether, and Other Vapors, to Surgical Operations*. He had copies of this pamphlet forwarded to

France and other countries, where it was read at medical and scientific societies.

Wells then gathered testimonials from his patients about his nitrous oxide work. These, too, he forwarded to France, but as he did so, Wells realized he had another problem beyond proving he had been first. Nitrous oxide was fine for taking out teeth, people insisted, but it wasn't good for capital operations like amputations of legs. People began to say that even if Wells had been first, he shouldn't be proclaimed as the discoverer of anesthesia.

In April Wells went to New York City to pick up his paintings that had been shipped from France, but he soon abandoned his plan to become an art dealer. Instead, he would become the first American to earn a living as an anesthetist, later called an anesthesiologist. He would determine whether nitrous oxide, ether, or a new anesthetic called chloroform was best in a particular case, then anesthetize the patient for the surgeon. While he was at it, he expected to prove that nitrous oxide was adequate for capital operations.

But how could Wells tell which anesthetic was best for various cases? He decided to once again experiment on himself and did so, in his Hartford office, which he had reopened in 1847. That year and in early 1848 he successfully anesthetized a number of his own dental patients as well as surgical patients undergoing serious operations. But at the same time, Wells slipped beyond scientific experimentation and began to crave anesthetics for his own use. When he breathed ether, nitrous oxide, or chloroform, he felt happy and without a care.

Horace Wells's last days were a whirlwind of activity. On New Year's Day of 1848 he administered nitrous oxide to a man before a leg amputation. Three days later he did the same for a woman who had a big tumor removed from her shoulder. Although medicine's final verdict was that nitrous oxide was too weak for capital operations, Wells felt that he was proving otherwise.

Wells figured that New York City was where he had the best opportunity to achieve fame as an anesthetist. He decided to go to New York alone, establish himself, then send for Elizabeth and Charles. Wells reached New York City around January 17, the day the New York *Evening Post* ran his notice saying that people seeking "advice respecting the use of Chloroform, Nitrous Oxide Gas, and Letheon" should visit him in his room at 120 Chambers Street.

Wells never could stand to be away from home, and he suffered unbearable pangs of loneliness in New York. To ease the pain he inhaled ether and chloroform with increasing frequency. He walked the city's streets just to be with people, sneaking breaths from a bottle hidden in his pocket. Soon he was in a perpetual stupor in which he was never certain whether he was in his room dreaming, or walking the pavement.

We know the basic facts of Horace Wells's last few days, but the reasons for what he did remain a mystery. On the night of January 21, 1848, his thirty-third birthday, Wells went out with a chloroform bottle and a bottle of acid. Staggering along Broadway, he spotted two prostitutes and sprinkled acid on their clothing. According to one story, the women had earlier sprinkled acid on a derelict Wells had befriended on one of his walks. The man told Wells about it, and he took revenge on behalf of his friend.

Fortunately the women were not burned by the acid, but Horace Wells was arrested and locked in Tombs Prison, where he continued to inhale chloroform and ether. From time to time when his mind cleared he realized that he had sunk lower than he had ever thought possible. Wells wrote several letters from prison, including a heartbreaking farewell message to his family:

> *Sunday evening, 7 o'clock*
> *Great God! Has it come to this? Is it not all a*
> *dream? Before 12 o'clock this night I am to pay the*

debt of Nature. Yes, if I was to go free tomorrow, I could not live and be called a villain. God knows I am not one. O, my dear mother, brother, and sister, what can I say to you? My anguish will only allow me to bid you farewell. I die tonight, believing that God, who knoweth all hearts, will forgive the dreadful act. I shall spend my remaining time in prayer.

Oh! what misery I shall bring upon all my near relatives, and what still more distresses me is the fact that my name is familiar to the whole scientific world, as being connected with an important discovery; and now, while I am scarcely able to hold my pen, I must bid all farewell! May God forgive me! Oh! my dear wife and child, whom I leave destitute of the means of support—I would still live and work for you, but I cannot—for were I to live on, I should become a maniac. I feel that I am but little better than one already. The instrument of my destruction was obtained when the officer who had me in charge kindly permitted me to go to my room yesterday.

Horace Wells

That Sunday night, January 23, Horace Wells breathed an unusually large dose of chloroform. Nearly unconscious, the man who had often run from his problems before now did so in the most extreme way. Early on the morning of the twenty-fourth, Horace Wells slashed his left thigh with his razor and bled to death.

It is believed that the story of Horace Wells lives on in one of the most famous tales in literature. Robert Louis Stevenson's 1886 novel, *The Strange Case of Dr. Jekyll and Mr. Hyde*—about a doctor who takes a drug that turns him into a maniac—was said to have been inspired by the life and death of Horace Wells.

This picture showing the death of Horace Wells is highly fictionalized; he actually died in bed, not in a bathtub.

As Horace Wells was being buried at Hartford's Old North Burying Ground, his wife sadly commented, "My husband's great gift which he devoted to the service of mankind proved a curse to himself and his family." Had he been able to face life a little while longer, Wells would have seen the tide turning in his favor in some circles. Just a few days after his death, word came from France that the Paris Medical Society had voted Horace Wells the discoverer of anesthesia.

For sixty years Horace Wells lay in Hartford's Old North Burying Ground, where Elizabeth had joined him in 1889 at the age of seventy-one. Then in 1908 Charles removed his parents' remains to Cedar Hill Cemetery, a beautiful place of woods and ponds where Hartford's "better" people spend eternity. Near his father's grave, Charles erected a magnificent monument that honors his contribution to anesthesia. The front shows an angel bringing a potion to a patient who is reclining on the words THERE SHALL BE NO PAIN. The back of the monument contains a simple inscription Wells would have liked:

HORACE WELLS
1815–1848
DISCOVERER OF ANESTHESIA

CHAPTER IX

THE "BENEFACTORS OF MANKIND"

By late 1847 William Morton realized that there would be no fortune from his ether patent. He was only able to keep Etherton and feed his family through generous gifts from his friends. But instead of rebuilding his dental practice, which Jackson had damaged, Morton began a new quest.

Governments occasionally reward people for great discoveries or inventions. The British government awarded Edward Jenner thirty thousand pounds in the early 1800s for his discovery of a vaccination against smallpox. The United States government awarded Robert Fulton's heirs $76,300 for his pioneering work on the steamboat. On November 20, 1847, Dr. John Warren, Dr. George Hayward, and others at Massachusetts General Hospital sent a petition to the United States Senate and House of Representatives asking the government to investigate and then reward the discoverer or discoverers of anesthesia. The petitioners didn't name Morton, for they didn't want to appear to be acting solely in his behalf, yet they were confident that a government investigation would decide in Morton's favor.

In France, too, there was a large monetary prize to be won. Now and then the French Academy of Sciences awarded what was called the Montyon Prize to a "Benefactor of Mankind." Winning the Montyon and United States awards could still make Morton wealthy and also convince the world that he, not Jackson, was the discoverer.

William Morton began preparing his "proofs" to help his chances of winning the awards. He spent hundreds of hours writing papers and collecting statements from patients, doctors, and eyewitnesses. Photocopy machines did not yet exist, so Morton had to copy all the statements by hand and have them signed. When completed, the material he sent to Paris occupied five trunks. The documents he assembled in anticipation of a United States government investigation were roughly equal in bulk. By neglecting his dental practice to prepare these proofs, Morton fell so deeply into debt that he began to view the prizes as his only means of salvation.

Several months after it first appeared in Paris, *Morton's Memoir* was reprinted in America in the March 1848 *Littell's Living Age*. From Frances Long Taylor's biography of her father we know that Crawford Long subscribed to *Littell's,* in the pages of which he may have learned details about William Morton's work. Finding that Morton's first public demonstration of anesthesia, the Gilbert Abbott operation, had taken place on October 16, 1846, Long calculated that his operation on James Venable had occurred four and a half years earlier. Had he published anything on his work during that time, Long realized, the discovery would have been his and his alone.

Crawford Long wasn't one to envy those who won glory that might have been his. He was happy that the world now had a way to prevent surgical pain, and blamed no one but himself for missing the opportunity to receive credit for the discovery. Still, he agreed with his friends: The world should know that he had been first, and he should apply for the award that the government seemed sure to make to the discoverer.

But there were still babies to deliver and sick people to treat, so more months passed before Long produced an article. His kindly nature shone through in his essay that finally appeared in the December 1849 *Southern Medical and Surgical Journal*. He mentioned the clash between Morton, Jackson, and Wells without any bitterness toward their claims of being first, while admitting his own "negligence" for not presenting his case earlier. He then recounted how the idea occurred to him at an ether frolic, described the James Venable operation, and presented signed statements from Venable and witnesses to the operation. Long closed with typical modesty: "I leave it with an enlightened medical profession, to say, whether or not my claim to the discovery of etherization is forfeited, by not being presented earlier, and with the decision which may be made, I shall be content."

Within a month of his article's publication, Long sold his home and office in Jefferson, and moved his family to Atlanta, where he developed a large medical practice. But in 1851, missing familiar surroundings, the family moved to Athens, where Long had attended college. Besides working as a physician in Athens, Crawford Long established a drugstore that grew into northeast Georgia's largest medicine business.

At first Long's anesthesia article received scant attention outside Georgia. As he had expected, his extensive delay had hurt his chances for recognition. True to his word, Long was "content" with this decision. Crawford Long was a contented man, pleased with his medical work and with the new babies Caroline and he added to their family roughly every eighteen months over the next few years.

Like Crawford Long, Charles Jackson had a life beyond the anesthesia controversy. Many geologists and chemists considered Jackson a genius in their fields without knowing much about his involvement in this conflict. Yet an event proved that even while Jackson was writing "Remarks on the Structure of Ice and Glaciers" or investigating a mineral deposit far from home, his quest for recognition as the discoverer of anesthesia boiled in his head.

In 1847 the United States government appointed Jackson to survey the public lands around Lake Superior in what is now Michigan's Upper Peninsula. Generally Dr. Jackson enjoyed his geological expeditions, but the anesthesia dispute had just begun and he was disturbed at being sent a thousand miles from the scene of the action in Boston.

Jackson's assistants on this survey included twenty-seven–year-old Josiah Whitney, a geologist who had much in common with William Morton. Not only were they the same age, but Whitney had lived in Jackson's home while studying geology with him in 1841–1842.

Whitney was flattered to accompany his former teacher on the Michigan expedition, but once they reached camp in the north woods, Jackson ordered Whitney and his six other assistants to do all the work, while he remained in the tent, writing letters to scientists about the anesthesia controversy. Jackson was drinking heavily by this time, which made the situation worse. In the evenings he sat around the campfire complaining drunkenly about how he had been robbed of all of his discoveries.

Besides making it clear that he considered the geological survey a petty business compared to the anesthesia controversy, Jackson pocketed government funds that were meant for the assistants. Josiah Whitney and another assistant became so disgusted that they sent their resignations to the United States interior secretary with a list of Jackson's wrongdoings. Jackson resigned from the expedition, but later informed government officials that his mutinous assistants had forced this upon him. Unable to determine exactly what had happened in the wilds of Michigan, the government reinstated Jackson's good standing as a geologist. Jackson then waged a campaign to smear Whitney's reputation, perhaps failing only because most of his venom was directed against William Morton at the time.

Whitney went on to eclipse his ex-teacher as a geologist, and in 1864 measured what was the nation's highest mountain until Alaska joined the country. This California peak was named Mount Whitney in his honor.

Jackson returned from Michigan to find that decisions on anesthesia were coming in. Massachusetts General Hospital named Morton the discoverer, and gave him a one-thousand-dollar prize, which briefly eased his poverty. The hospital's decision was expected, for Morton's triumphs had occurred there. Likewise, no one was surprised when the Connecticut legislature named Wells as the discoverer and the Georgia Medical Association gave the honor to Long. Overseas, Germany and Turkey acclaimed Jackson as the discoverer, while Russia and Sweden gave the nod to Morton.

William Morton had some extremely bad luck in France. In early 1849 he learned that his five trunkfuls of papers had never reached the scientists in Paris. Morton had asked Christopher Brewster, the American dentist living in Paris, to distribute the papers. But Brewster still hoped that France would decide in favor of Wells (whom he had introduced to the French scientific societies) and award the prize money to Horace's widow, so he had left Morton's trunks unopened.

Disappointed and puzzled at not hearing any reaction from France about his documents, Morton wrote repeatedly to Brewster. Finally Brewster answered that he didn't have time to distribute the papers and that it was too late anyway. "My advice would be to sell them as old paper," he informed Morton about the precious proofs he had sent off three years earlier.

Without Morton's papers to help his cause, the French government named Jackson the discoverer. He was awarded the French Legion of Honor medal, which he proudly wore pinned over his heart on special occasions. But *Morton's Memoir,* which had been published in Paris, impressed the French Academy of Sciences. The academy awarded the Montyon Prize to both Jackson and Morton as codiscoverers. The five thousand francs that came with the award was to be divided between the two men.

Jackson accepted his half. But Morton felt so bitter toward Jackson that he refused the 2,500 francs (now equal to about 10,500 dollars) even though it would have eased his family's poverty. Since Morton wouldn't accept the money, the academy used the 2,500 francs to make a gold medal in a gold frame for him. Jackson had a jealous fit when he learned that his enemy had received a medal saying *Academy of Sciences: Montyon Prize for Medicine and Surgery: 1847–1848: William T. G. Morton,* and went around Boston saying that the Montyon Prize was his alone and that "Morton has caused by his own order a medal to be made for him by some jeweler or goldsmith of Paris."

But the biggest prize—at least as far as money was concerned—was still to come. By 1852 Congress was considering an award to the discoverer of anesthesia. And what an award! Determined to show the world how proud they were of what everyone was calling "the greatest discovery ever made in the United States," the lawmakers settled on a prize of $100,000, equal to nearly two million dollars in today's money.

Collections were taken up for William Morton so that he could go to Washington, D.C., to plead his case to the lawmakers. Armed with his proofs, Morton went to the nation's capital, where everything went smoothly at first. Secretary of State Daniel Webster was so impressed by Morton that he took him along to government banquets, and by the middle of the year United States House and Senate committees had recommended that Morton be given the $100,000—provided that he turn over his etherization patent to the government. This was agreeable to Morton, who wasn't getting anything from the patent anyway. But another step was needed before the money was his. The House and Senate could pass a bill granting Morton the reward, or the president, as commander of the armed forces, could request that the government issue the reward because the military needed Morton's technique. From the talk around Capitol Hill, Morton felt that it was just a matter of time before the government paid him the $100,000 one way or the other. Jackson was also pelting the lawmakers with proofs, however, so Morton borrowed more money in order to remain for long periods in the nation's capital lobbying for the reward. Yet when things began to unravel for Morton, Jackson wasn't the reason.

By August of 1852 Horace Wells had more boosters for his cause in Connecticut than he had ever had while alive. There was a growing outcry from the Nutmeg State that Horace Wells had been the true trailblazer and that Boston was trying to steal his glory. Sympathy for Wells's wife and son added to the clamor. Horace's suicide had left Elizabeth and young Charles impoverished. Wells's foot-pumped shower bath, Panorama of Nature, traveling singing-canaries show, venture in French paintings, anesthesia work, and in the end his neglected dental career were all financial disasters. The only items of value Wells left—his office furniture and dental tools—were auctioned to pay his debts. Their total value was only $166.37, including 978 false teeth worth $58.68 and a dentist's chair valued at $3.00. Their home in Hartford also had to be sold, forcing Elizabeth and Charles to move in with friends or relatives.

Wells's boosters asked their legislators in Washington, D.C., to seek the $100,000 for Elizabeth and Charles. Incredibly, Jackson even took up Wells's cause—at least temporarily. He met with Elizabeth Wells and with Connecticut lawmakers, explained that Wells and he were the real discoverers of anesthesia, and offered to give up his share of the $100,000 to Horace's wife and son.

On August 28, 1852, the Senate was discussing Morton's $100,000 award. One senator after another spoke in praise of William Morton when suddenly Connecticut's Truman Smith leaped to his feet. "I denounce this attempt to filch money from the Treasury," Senator Smith angrily said. "I demand, in the name of justice and right, to have an opportunity to come before the Señate, and tell the story of the wrongs of the poor widow and defenseless children of Dr. Wells—wrongs which they have suffered at the hands of this man, Morton, who has attempted to rob their husband and father who has descended into the grave." Actually, there was just one child, but Senator Smith had used the plural to make the family's plight seem all the more tragic.

Being accused of robbing a widow and fatherless boy wasn't something the sixty-two senators representing the nation's thirty-one states could ignore. Several objected that Senator Smith was making a last-second attempt to confuse the issue, but, as Jackson had hoped, doubt crept into the minds of many others. They didn't want to hand Morton $100,000, only to learn later that it should have gone to Wells's family. The legislature planned more committee studies to examine the evidence Wells had compiled before his death.

Jackson found a way to further confuse the issue. He had read Crawford Long's article in the December 1849 *Southern Medical and Surgical Journal,* still little known outside Georgia in 1854. Jackson wrote to Georgia senator William Dawson, saying that Long's claim deserved study. Dawson answered that Jackson himself should conduct an investigation.

About twenty-five years earlier, gold had been found in northern Georgia, prompting the United States government to set up a mint in the town of Dahlonega. In 1854 Jackson arranged for the United States government to send him to inspect the Georgia gold mines. The trip from Boston to Dahlonega was a difficult one thousand miles by train and stagecoach, but Jackson's real goal—the town of Athens—was only another seventy miles by stagecoach.

Early on the morning of March 8, 1854, a stranger entered Dr. Crawford W. Long's drugstore in Athens. An employee and student of Long's named Charles Andrews answered the door. "Dr. Long is not in, but I think he will be, in a short time," said Andrews, inviting the stranger to sit by the fire. In a letter he wrote about this incident, Andrews described the stranger as "a spare-made, angular man, of 5 feet 10 inches height, of swarthy complexion, with dark hair and eyes, and apparently 40 years of age."

Long entered his drugstore a few minutes later, and the stranger handed him a card that read:

CHARLES T. JACKSON, M.D.,
State Assayer
Analytic and Consulting Chemist,
Mineralogist and Geologist.
House and Office 32 Somerset Street, Boston

Excited and highly flattered by the famous scientist's visit, Crawford Long sat down to talk to him. "I have called for the purpose of comparing notes as to the discovery of ether anesthesia," Jackson said, "since both of us, and others, have claimed the discovery." Despite his respect for Jackson, Long knew a little about his habit of claiming other people's discoveries, so he asked his clerk Charles Andrews to make a record of their conversation.

Jackson then recounted his version of the discovery. "A few doors from my office in Boston is the office of Dr. William Morton, a dentist. On September 30, 1846, Dr. Morton came to my office and said, 'Dr. Jackson, I have to perform an operation upon a patient who is suffering very much, and is in a very nervous condition. Can you suggest, or give me something that will allay the pain, and quiet the nervousness?' I then took a vial of ether, and fully directed him how to have the patient inhale it." Jackson continued to distort the facts, depicting Morton as a puppet carrying out his ideas, yet admitting his own involvement in a dispute with Morton and Wells's heirs over the $100,000 government award. "But now it has become known to us that you used ether as an anesthetic in 1842," continued Jackson. "I would like to examine your evidence as to the discovery."

Long excused himself and drove his buggy the few blocks to his home on Waddell Street. Eight-year-old Frances was playing by the fireplace when her father rushed in and she followed him up to the attic. Seventy-four years later, in her biography of her father, Frances explained, "He unlocked a little green traveling trunk, took from it a package of papers, rushed back to his buggy, and was driven rapidly away."

Caroline Long warned her curious daughter, "Never play with the papers in this trunk, for the contents mean too much to your father. They will make him a great man someday."

Long returned to the drugstore, where he and Dr. Jackson pored over the signed statements and letters. Finally, Jackson explained that he had geological business in Dahlonega, but would return in a few days. Long gave Jackson names of people who had witnessed his etherizing patients in Jefferson, where the stagecoach would make a lunch stop on the way to Dahlonega.

Ten days later, Jackson returned to Long's office. Long had been first to use anesthesia, Jackson admitted, but added that publishing his results so late had damaged his chances. "Let us share the honor and benefits of the discovery," Jackson offered, "for you have the advantage of being first, while we have the advantage in having first published it to the world."

Long knew what "sharing the benefits" meant. If he cooperated with Jackson in winning the award from Congress, the two of them could split the $100,000. But Long wasn't the kind of man to exclude Morton and Wells by making a secret deal with Jackson. "My claim to the discovery and use of ether as an anesthetic rests upon the facts of my use of it on the thirtieth March 1842," Crawford Long explained in refusing Jackson's deal, "of which I have indisputable evidence."

Using Long to defeat Morton, then sharing the $100,000 with the pleasant country doctor, would have been gratifying to Jackson. But now that this plan had failed, he put another plan into effect. In the interest of fairness, he told Long, he wanted to help place his claims before Congress. Crawford Long agreed to Jackson's seemingly unselfish offer.

Upon his return home, Jackson wrote to Georgia senator William Dawson saying that Dr. Crawford Williamson Long was fully entitled to the $100,000 award. On April 15, 1854, when the Senate was again debating the anesthesia prize, William Dawson took the floor and read from Jackson's letter in which he withdrew from the contest in favor of Dr. Long.

Hatred for Morton wasn't the sole reason Jackson suddenly went into Long's corner. Jackson might be out of the running for the $100,000, but he still had a chance for something far dearer to him—going down in history as the discoverer of anesthesia. Of his three opponents, Jackson felt, Long's case was the weakest. Jackson planned to use Long to knock Morton and Wells out of contention, then later defeat Long on the grounds that he had published his results too late. This would leave only one man standing at the end—Dr. Charles Thomas Jackson!

But Jackson left nothing to chance. Fearing that history might side with Long, he decided to show that he had etherized a patient—himself—more than a month before Long's James Venable operation. According to Jackson's story, one day in February of 1842 he had nearly choked to death while preparing a model volcano. To clear his lungs, he breathed from a bottle of ether. The next morning his throat was very sore, so he decided to breathe ether again. He sat down in his rocking chair, soaked a towel in a bottle of ether, and placed it over his nose and mouth. When Jackson awoke more than fifteen minutes later (as he later wrote), "the idea flashed into my mind

*An artist's version of Dr. Jackson's story that he etherized
himself in February 1842*

that I had made the discovery I had for so long a time been in quest of—a means of rendering [a patient] temporarily insensible, so as to admit of the performance of a surgical operation." Jackson went on to explain that he did "numerous carefully conducted experiments," including "experiments on my own person," before having his assistant, Morton, etherize patients.

Even if Jackson had etherized himself as he claimed, he concocted the February 1842 date to make it seem like the incident occurred before the Venable operation. The young geologist Josiah Whitney had been living at Jackson's in February 1842, and he reported that the rocking-chair incident never occurred, nor had he seen the slightest evidence of Jackson's "numerous experiments" with ether. In one way it would be a relief to find that Jackson actually did etherize himself repeatedly, for it might help explain his Jekyll and Hyde personality. However, it is likely that the only "patients" Jackson ever etherized were animals. In one case that Jackson wrote up in 1852, he claimed to have etherized a pet mountain lion that belonged to a friend. As the animal slept, Jackson cut off its claws so that, as he explained, "the animal should not be able to injure [the friend's] children."

Crawford Long never promoted his claims in Congress, but Senator Dawson and other Southern lawmakers did so for him. By 1855 a kind of civil war was raging over the anesthesia discovery. Generally Southerners sided with Crawford Long, and Northerners with Morton, Wells, or Jackson, but there were other subdivisions. Massachusetts people favored Morton or Jackson, Vermonters and Connecticuters boosted Wells, dentists rooted for Wells or Morton, doctors pulled for Long or Jackson (except in New England, where a great many were for Morton), pharmacists supported Long, while geologists and chemists lined up behind Jackson. The members of the United States Congress unquestionably favored Morton. Yet, overwhelmed by a flood of opinions and a mountain of "proofs," they met again and again without granting him the reward.

By this time Morton's health was failing. On some days he couldn't get out of bed, because, as he wrote to a friend, "my limbs tremble and I feel dizzy, weak, and despondingly sick." He added that "my nervous system seems so completely shattered that a surprise or a sudden noise sends a shock all over me. I am so restless that I cannot lie or sit long in any position, day or night. Convulsive pains seize me suddenly without any warning or apparent cause, and my limbs are instantly drawn up by the cramps which wrack me so that I cannot prevent screaming until I fall exhausted."

The pressure of lobbying for himself in Washington as his debts mounted contributed to Morton's physical and mental collapse. His ether experiments over the years were also a factor in his poor health. Scientists now know that the repeated inhaling of drugs like ether over long periods can harm the body's organs, including the brain, as Horace Wells had so tragically demonstrated.

Several times William Morton came agonizingly close to winning the award. The closest was in the spring of 1855. William Henry Witte, a United States representative from Pennsylvania who lived near Morton's rented room in Washington, D.C., befriended Morton and spoke to President Franklin Pierce on his behalf. "I will talk it over with the Secretary of War and see what is the best plan," President Pierce told Witte. "I will see him tonight so that I can give you an answer tomorrow." Witte was so certain that Morton's $100,000 was as good as on its way that he joined the long list of people who lent him money.

Two days later—March 23, 1855—Witte returned for the president's answer. The news seemed to be great. On the president's desk was a petition from Massachusetts General Hospital, plus reports from the Smithsonian Institution and various congressional committees, all recommending that Morton receive the award. Also on the desk was the paper that would grant Morton the $100,000, once the president signed it. Franklin Pierce picked up his pen and was just starting to sign his name when he suddenly froze.

"There is a point which is not yet exactly clear to my mind, as to whether the patent includes all anesthetic substances—for instance, chloroform," said the president, setting down his pen. "For a little information on the subject, and to prevent any more doubt, I think I will refer it to the Attorney General so that I can find out exactly what the patent does cover." The president feared that if the government gave Morton $100,000 for his ether patent, it would have to do the same for other anesthetics. Tell Morton that he needn't worry, President Pierce reassured Witte. The matter would soon be resolved one way or another in his favor.

William Morton returned to Etherton to await the good news the president had promised. During that summer of 1855, he turned his attention to farmwork, which helped him recover some of his health. In the fall, Morton entered the Norfolk County Fair and won seventy dollars for having the finest dairy herd, five dollars for Beauty his milk cow, and another five dollars for his geese. But the year ended and 1856 began, and still Morton had not heard from the president.

William Henry Witte wrote to President Pierce, pleading with him in the name of justice to award William Morton the $100,000. Finally, the president agreed to meet with Morton in May 1856, fourteen months after he had promised "an answer tomorrow." The president had no $100,000 check for Morton, but he did offer a new plan. Morton must sue the United States government for using his patented ether technique without compensating him. It would be a charade they would all act out, the president explained. Morton would sue, the government would lose, then pay him the $100,000. Morton could even choose which government facility to sue.

Morton's lawyers selected the Marine Hospital near Boston along with a doctor there, Charles Davis, as the targets of their lawsuit. The lawyers visited Dr. Davis to assure him that the suit was a mere formality orchestrated by the president in order to reward William Morton the $100,000. Besides suing this government hospital, the lawyers also sued a private firm, the New York Eye Infirmary, for infringing Morton's patent.

The New York Eye Infirmary fought the lawsuit. With the help of a new friend, Dr. Davis did so, too. Charles T. Jackson visited the Marine Hospital and filled Dr. Charles Davis's mind with questions. Thousands of doctors were using ether, so why should he be the one to be sued? What if the government abandoned him once he lost the suit? The result was that Davis hired his own lawyers to fight Morton's suit.

Most people didn't know that the president had urged the lawsuits as a device for Morton to obtain the $100,000, and concluded that the dentist was trying to prevent doctors from using ether unless they paid him. The American Medical Association officially condemned Morton at a meeting in New York City, and much of the public viewed him as a greedy villain. One day some neighborhood children made a dummy that resembled William Morton and set it ablaze in front of Etherton. The entire neighborhood gathered to watch the effigy go up in flames as the Morton children screamed in terror.

Morton had far worse problems. By 1856, he had not practiced dentistry for about ten years and was perhaps $50,000 in debt. Sensing that Morton would never get the $100,000, people who had loaned him money rushed to demand repayment. He would have lost Etherton if friends hadn't bought it and allowed him and his family to live there rent-free. As it was, Morton had to sell the family piano, his children's pony, and many other belongings. The situation became so desperate for the Mortons that at times the family had only tattered clothing to wear and not enough to eat.

One day in about 1856 a Boston pawnbroker was in his shop when a shaking hand thrust a large medal under his window. Testing it, the pawnbroker found that the medal was gold. However, he was troubled by the inscription: *Academy of Sciences: Montyon Prize for Medicine and Surgery: 1847–1848: William T. G. Morton.* Thinking that the trembling, sickly-looking man had stolen the medal, the pawnbroker asked him for identification.

After studying the crumpled paper that had come with the medal, the pawnbroker realized that this was actually William Morton before him. "Are you absolutely obliged to pawn this medal, Dr. Morton?" the pawnbroker asked.

"I have no choice. It is the last thing of value I possess, and I can no longer buy food for my wife and children."

But even pawning the medal was not the worst of it. To buy his family bread, he began gathering wood in the forest, which he sold from a handcart. Friends who learned of Morton's plight arranged for a number of testimonial dinners at which money was raised for him in tribute to his discovery. One of the groups that raised money for Morton was called "Patrons of Science and the Friends of Humanity." Massachusetts General Hospital also awarded him another thousand dollars. Thanks to the fund-raisings, Morton could at least feed and clothe his family and reclaim his medal and other belongings. Yet he knew that these collections, which he depended upon for the rest of his life, were little more than charity.

In 1857, the year his and Elizabeth's fifth and last child was born, William nearly grasped the big prize once more. It appears that James Buchanan, the president after Pierce, wanted Morton to have the money, but treasury secretary Howell Cobb either talked him out of it or even refused the president's order to issue the $100,000 check. Cobb had reason to oppose Morton. A member of a famous Georgia family (which also produced baseball legend Ty Cobb), Howell Cobb had been born the same year as Crawford Long in a nearby county, and had been his classmate at the University of Georgia.

William Morton's lawsuits—his last hope for winning the $100,000—were decided on December 1, 1862. The judge heaped praise on Morton. "Distinguished surgeons agree in ranking it among the great discoveries of modern times," he said. "You are entitled to be classed among the great benefactors of mankind." The word Morton dreaded the most came next. "But," the judge continued, "the beneficent character of the discovery cannot change the legal principles on which the law of patents is founded. A discovery is not patentable."

During the fifteen years since Massachusetts General Hospital had first petitioned Congress, Morton had frequently heard himself praised, only to have some "but" snatch the prize away. This "but" was the final blow. Discovering that ether could be used as an anesthetic was a great service to humanity, the judge was saying, but it wasn't patentable because ether had been known for centuries.

As if to further taunt William Morton, in 1863 his boosters in Congress proposed that his prize be raised to $200,000. Six separate legislative committees had recommended Morton for the reward, they argued, so it was time for Congress to vote in his favor. But the judge's decision on his patent had ended Morton's cause in many legislators' minds. In 1863 the reward issue died out forever in Congress, which by then had a far more serious matter to contend with—the Civil War.

CHAPTER X

THE BATTLE TO THE DEATH, PART II

Charles Jackson's visit stirred Crawford Long's feelings about the anesthesia controversy, as did the Georgian's failure to win the reward in Congress. Earlier Crawford Long had managed to ward off pangs of regret, but now his children sometimes found him sitting by his little green trunk, studying his ether documents. "Father is attacked by the old fever," the children would say. And once when Caroline predicted "The day will come when you will be recognized as the discoverer of ether anesthesia," her husband answered, "Never mention the word *anesthesia* to me again!"

Long received a boost from Charles Jackson as late as 1861. Still worried that Congress would decide in Morton's favor, Jackson wrote an article about Long called "First Practical Use of Ether in Surgical Operations" for the April 11 *New England Journal of Medicine*. There was no worse time in the nation's history for this article to have appeared. The next day, April 12, 1861, the Civil War began, largely over the issue of the South continuing to allow slavery. With Georgia on the Southern side, there was no chance that the Union government would decide in Long's favor. Besides, with a war to fight, the government didn't have the time or money to continue the anesthesia controversy.

Although he owned slaves, Crawford Long deeply loved his country and thought the conflict between the North and South could be resolved without war. His old University of Georgia roommate, Alexander Stephens, shared his feelings. Yet once the war began, both men remained loyal to their state and to the South. Stephens was chosen vice president of the Confederacy, while Long was placed in charge of a Confederate hospital in Athens.

Long's foresight in ordering huge amounts of ether, chloroform, and other medical materials as the war began saved many lives, for he was able to treat patients after other Southern hospitals ran out of supplies. Besides tending to Confederate troops and their families at the hospital, Long cared for wounded Northern soldiers who had been captured. We don't have an exact count, but we know that Dr. Long performed many operations using anesthetics during the four years of the war.

By early 1864 it was apparent that the South would be defeated. One August morning that year, word reached Dr. Long that Union troops were nearby and would soon be heading for Athens. Unable to leave his hospital patients, Long sent a soldier on crutches with a message for Caroline and the children. They must load the family valuables into their carriage and hide them at the wounded soldier's farm.

His family was still packing when Long reached home. Since the Yankees wouldn't be suspicious of young people, he wanted the two oldest of his seven children, eighteen-year-old Frances and twelve-year-old Edward, to hide the valuables. Long removed the documents from the green trunk and placed them in a large glass jar, which he gave to Frances. "These are the proofs of my discovery of ether anesthesia," he told her. "When you reach your destination bury them in a secluded spot. But if overtaken by the raiders, you may give them the jar if ordered to do so."

"I will die before I do!" answered Frances, swelling with pride over the importance of her mission. Once at the wounded soldier's farm, Frances buried the jar in the woods, covering the spot with leaves and sticks.

The Northerners were stopped from invading Athens on this occasion, but they seized the town when the war ended in the spring of 1865. Crawford Long was hired by the federal government at forty dollars a month to treat injured and sick Union soldiers stationed in Athens after the war. By the end of 1865, the Union troops departed from Athens, but Union forces remained in other parts of Georgia until 1870. Then, satisfied that Georgia had freed its slaves and granted the ex-slaves their voting and other rights, the soldiers left, and Georgia was readmitted to the United States. By then Frances had dug up the jar with the papers and returned them to her father.

Charles Jackson's life was little disturbed by the Civil War. No longer a practicing physician, he was not asked to serve the Union, nor did he volunteer. Instead, he spent the four years of the conflict making geological expeditions and devoting more and more time to his anesthesia claims. Fifty-six years old when the war began, he craved a place in history more than ever before. In 1861, the same year in which he wrote the article giving the credit to Long, he also published *A Manual of Etherization,* a book in which he claimed the discovery for himself. Most of his published articles on etherization also appeared during the war years—while Morton and Long were busy with other matters.

William Morton's wartime experiences were similar to Crawford Long's, only he served on the Northern side as a volunteer battlefield anesthetist in Virginia. On December 13, 1862, just twelve days after the judge ruled that "a discovery is not patentable," Morton served at the Battle of Fredericksburg. Then in the spring of 1864 he volunteered at the Battle of the Wilderness, at which a famous doctor from

Philadelphia recorded an incident concerning him.

Dr. John Brinton was at the headquarters of General Ulysses S. Grant, recently named commander of Union forces by President Abraham Lincoln, when an aide approached with a request. A volunteer medical worker waiting nearby wanted a horse-drawn ambulance in which to visit the wounded. General Grant answered that all the ambulances were needed by official army personnel, and that none could be spared. The aide reported the bad news to the volunteer, whom Dr. Brinton recognized as William Morton, "a travel-stained man, in brownish clothes." Brinton asked Morton to wait a minute while he went to speak to Grant himself.

"General," said Brinton, "if you knew who that man is, I think you would give him what he asks for."

"No, I will not divert an ambulance today for anyone," snapped the general. "They are all required elsewhere."

"General, he has done so much for mankind, so much for the soldier, and you will say so when you know his name," Brinton persisted.

General Grant removed his cigar from his mouth and asked, "Who is he?"

"Dr. Morton, the discoverer of ether."

Brinton reported that the general paused, then said, "You are right, doctor, let him have the ambulance and anything else he wants."

During the war William Morton anesthetized more than two thousand soldiers, many of whom underwent amputations of mangled legs or arms. Sometimes Morton and the doctors he worked with had a house for a hospital, but often the surgery was performed in a tent or out in the open under a tree. In a letter to a friend, Morton wrote, "I prepared the patients for the knife, producing anesthesia in an average time of three minutes. The surgeons followed, performing their operations with dexterous skill, while the dressers in their turn bound up the stumps." But even working far into the night by torchlight, they could not attend all the wounded, so that some soldiers with more serious wounds were left to die. The Civil War, which cost more American lives than any other war in history, mercifully ended in April of 1865.

The hardships of war improved William Morton's health, probably because they took his mind off the anesthesia dispute. But his nervous attacks resumed once he returned to Etherton. His trembling, dizziness, convulsive pains, and sleeplessness turned Morton's life into a living hell. With the $100,000 reward withdrawn, Morton, like Charles Jackson, made it his sole purpose in life to go down in history as the discoverer of anesthesia. When his health permitted, he scoured the medical journals and popular magazines, searching for references to anesthesia.

One day Morton came across an article entitled "The Discovery of Etherization" in the June 1868 *Atlantic Monthly*. He was gravely disappointed that the author sided with Jackson, especially since the magazine was published in Boston, the city most solidly on Morton's side. So disturbed was Morton that he decided to go to New York City to present the magazines there with his version of the story.

Although Elizabeth and his doctor advised against it, William left Etherton for New York on July 6. Five days later, Elizabeth received an urgent telegram from New York. Her husband was ill and wanted her by his side. When Elizabeth arrived, she found that a doctor was treating her husband for pains he called rheumatism, and that the symptoms had somewhat subsided. Morton still planned to meet with magazine editors once he felt better.

A relative of Elizabeth's lent them a carriage during their stay in New York City. That summer was very hot, and after supper on the night of July 15, 1868, Morton suggested that they change to a hotel in a part of Manhattan that might be cooler. William Morton was driving the carriage across Central Park when suddenly he complained of feeling sleepy. When Elizabeth asked him to give her the reins to the horse or turn the carriage around, he refused. A short time later, without a word, he stopped the carriage and jumped out. For a moment he stared at Elizabeth in bewilderment. Then William Morton fell to the ground and quickly lost consciousness, suffering from a stroke.

A policeman and some passersby helped Elizabeth carry her husband onto the grass, "but he was past hope of recovery," Elizabeth later remembered. "The horror of the situation stunned me, finding myself alone with a dying husband, surrounded by strangers, in an open park at eleven o'clock at night." The policeman called for a larger carriage, but an hour passed before one arrived to take Morton to St. Luke's Hospital, where he was brought in on a stretcher.

When the doctors gathered around the patient, the chief surgeon recognized him. "This is Dr. Morton?" he asked Elizabeth.

"Yes," she said.

After a short silence the chief surgeon looked down at the dead body of forty-eight–year-old William Morton and said, "Young gentlemen, you see lying before you a man who has done more for humanity and for the relief of suffering than any man who has ever lived."

Elizabeth had removed her husband's prized possessions from his pocket at the park: his Montyon medal and his medals from Russia and Sweden. She laid them beside her husband's body, and said through her tears, "Yes, and here is all he has ever received for it!"

Morton's family buried him in Mount Auburn Cemetery, near Boston in Cambridge. Some doctors and other citizens of Boston erected an impressive monument over his grave, with an inscription written by Dr. Jacob Bigelow of Harvard Medical School and Massachusetts General Hospital.

One might think that Charles Jackson would take advantage of William Morton's death to vault into first place in the struggle for recognition, but the opposite occurred. People began to say how tragic it was that a great man like Morton had been hounded to death by Jackson. And, strangely, there is no record of Jackson ever writing another word about anes-

Charles Jackson in his later years

thesia after Morton's death. As Jackson's writing tapered off, his alcoholism became more of a problem.

On a July day five years after Morton's death, Dr. Jackson drunkenly made his way to Mount Auburn Cemetery. He found William Morton's grave, and studied the inscription on the monument:

WM. T. G. MORTON,
**INVENTOR AND REVEALER OF
ANESTHETIC INHALATION,
BORN AUGUST 9, 1819, DIED JULY 15, 1868.
ERECTED BY CITIZENS OF BOSTON.**

Standing there reading this inscription, Dr. Jackson went mad on the spot. His yells attracted the attention of visitors to the cemetery, who found him kicking and screaming like a baby throwing a tantrum. It has long been assumed that Jackson went insane because he felt that the words etched in marble crediting Morton as the "inventor and revealer of anesthetic inhalation" would be the verdict of history. A kinder thought is that at long last Jackson felt remorse for his persecution of William Morton.

Dr. Charles Jackson was taken to McLean Asylum in Somerville, outside Boston, where he spent the rest of his life. Jackson never published anything more, and we know absolutely nothing of what he may have said or done in his last seven years. He died at the McLean Asylum on August 28, 1880, at the age of seventy-five. His wife Susan buried him in Mount Auburn Cemetery, not far from William Morton's grave, beneath a stone inscribed:

CHARLES THOMAS JACKSON, M.D.
JUNE 21, 1805–AUGUST 28, 1880
**EMINENT AS A CHEMIST, MINERALOGIST, GEOLOGIST.
THROUGH HIS OBSERVATIONS OF THE EFFECTS OF
ETHER ON THE NERVES OF SENSATION,
THE DISCOVERY OF PAINLESS SURGERY WAS MADE.**

There is something heartbreaking about visiting Morton's and Jackson's graves at Mount Auburn Cemetery. There they lie, one having suffered an early death and the other driven insane over a discovery that should have brought both men so much joy. If they could come back, would they see the error of their ways and join together to claim the discovery? Or would they resume the argument where they left off well over a century ago?

CHAPTER XI

AND ONE LIVED HAPPILY EVER AFTER

Horace Wells and William Morton were dead, and Charles Jackson was losing his mind, but Crawford Long continued his happy life in Athens, Georgia. Much of his life revolved around children. Although he treated a variety of injured and sick people, he delivered babies, his favorite medical work, until virtually the final moment of his life.

By 1870 the Long family included seven children, ranging in age from twenty-five–year-old Frances to seven-year-old Maude. Each evening they sat for an hour or two at the dinner table talking. Later, Crawford Long read Shakespeare, Dickens, and other authors aloud to his family by the fireside. He also entertained his family by reading aloud the humorous articles that he wrote under the name Billy Muckle for one of the Athens papers, the *Southern Watchman*.

Besides his other "firsts," Crawford Long installed Athens's first soda fountain in his drugstore. He sometimes brought home bottles of soda pop for his children to drink and spray on each other at what they called "soda water sprees."

Through a chain of circumstances, Crawford Long was

also partly responsible for a kind of soda that has become a part of Americana. In about 1872, thirteen-year-old Joseph Jacobs went to work in Crawford Long's drugstore. Besides teaching Joseph to make medicines, Long showed him how to operate the soda fountain and make the carbon dioxide gas that gave the soda its fizz. Joseph Jacobs grew up to be a well-known Atlanta pharmacist who, like his teacher, operated a soda fountain in his drugstore. In 1886, Jacobs Pharmacy in Atlanta introduced to the world a new carbonated beverage that had originally been concocted as a headache remedy. The drink was named Coca-Cola. Historians have pointed out that if Crawford Long hadn't trained Joseph Jacobs to become a pharmacist, the world might never have had Coca-Cola!

As far as the anesthesia discovery was concerned, for many years Long remained relatively unknown compared to the three other contestants. This changed somewhat in 1877, when Dr. J. Marion Sims published an article called "The Discovery of Anesthesia" in the *Virginia Medical Monthly*. Dr. Sims's article was the first major work that presented Long's accomplishments to the American medical profession, as well as the first work that credited all four men as the discoverers, rather than one or the other. The families of Long, Wells, Morton, and Jackson each "ought to receive at least one hundred thousand dollars," wrote Sims. "I propose that the whole medical profession—North, South, East, and West—unite in asking Congress, at its next session, to appropriate this sum, as an anesthesia fund, to be divided equally between the families of Long, Wells, Morton, and Jackson.... Let us, as Americans, rise above all party, all prejudice, all sectionalism, and demand of the government this appropriation for the great work accomplished by these martyrs to science and humanity." Unfortunately, Dr. Sims's plea was ignored.

Just as his proofs rested comfortably in his green trunk, the ether controversy rested easily in Long's mind once again, as it had before Charles Jackson's visit. If not a world-famous figure—if not even very well known among the general public of his own country—he was beloved around Athens. A great tribute to Crawford Long was the fact that many people loved and respected him decades after his death. For example, Charles Andrews, who worked for Long in the drugstore and who described the meeting with Jackson, wrote in his later years, "As my employer and instructor, he was gentle, patient, and painstaking in fitting me for the struggles and business of life." Joseph Jacobs's memories were similar. Working in the drugstore alongside Crawford's son Arthur, Joseph felt more like a member of the family than an employee.

By 1877, when he was sixty-two years old, Long's health was starting to fail. He suffered terribly from headaches, and always seemed to feel tired. Today we think that he was a victim of high blood pressure. Long thought about slowing down his medical practice, but there were always more babies to deliver and sick people to help. One of the last operations he performed was the amputation of a man's leg—under ether, of course. Just as Long was leaving the operation, two ladies came up to him and kissed him on the cheek. One thanked him for saving her life in a difficult childbirth. The other, Mrs. Lucretia McCleskey, thanked Long for saving her life twenty-one years earlier by removing a cancerous breast. With reminders like this, how could he retire? Crawford Long even had a saying for those who told him to slow down: "My profession is to me a ministry from God."

Finally, his family convinced him that he should at least take a vacation. He planned it for early 1878 but repeatedly put it off. Finally, Long made plans to take the family to the mountains in August, but this was one promise he was not able to keep.

Crawford Long acted strangely at dinner on the night of June 15, 1878. His family noticed that he did not want them to get up and leave the table. Frances later wrote that her father reminisced about the past and gave each of them a talk

*A portrait of an aging Crawford Long painted by his
daughter Emma*

about "life and its duties." After a long time, he finally rose
from the table and said, "No man ever had better children than
I have." These words proved to be his farewell to them.

The next day Crawford Long was called upon to deliver a
baby for the wife of a Georgia lawmaker. He had just brought
the new little girl into the world when he suddenly felt very ill
and collapsed. His last words were, "Care for the mother and
child first." Then Dr. Crawford Williamson Long died, the victim of a stroke.

Long was buried in Oconee Hill Cemetery in Athens. Ten

years later, after she was killed in a train wreck near San Antonio, Texas, Caroline was buried next to her husband. Crawford Long is the only one of the four men involved in the controversy without a monument over him proclaiming him the discoverer of anesthesia. The monument to him in Oconee Hill Cemetery simply says:

CRAWFORD WILLIAMSON LONG, M.D.
BORN NOVEMBER 1, 1815
DIED IN ATHENS, GEORGIA JUNE 16, 1878
"MY PROFESSION IS TO ME A MINISTRY FROM GOD"

CHAPTER XII

THE BATTLE CONTINUES

The passing of Charles Jackson, the last of the four contestants, in August of 1880, virtually sounded the death knell for his cause. Without Jackson to promote himself, his role in the discovery of anesthesia has been downplayed by nearly everyone who has studied the controversy since the late 1800s. But supporters of the other three men have continued the struggle through plaques, statues, speeches, resolutions, and even movies.

In 1864 the American Dental Association named Horace Wells, then dead for sixteen years, as the discoverer. The American Medical Association also gave the laurels to Wells six years later in 1870. "Resolved," proclaimed the AMA, "that the honor of the Discovery of practical Anesthesia is due to the late Dr. Horace Wells of Connecticut." That same year, the AMA presented a petition to the United States Senate and House of Representatives requesting that they name Wells as the discoverer. The petition was never acted upon. In 1875 the city of Hartford and the state of Connecticut erected a statue of Horace Wells that can be seen in Bushnell Park near the state

Hartford, Connecticut, artist Charles Noel Flagg painted this portrait of Horace Wells in 1899, fifty-one years after Wells's death.

capitol. The twenty-five–foot-tall statue bears the inscription:

HORACE WELLS
THE DISCOVERER OF ANESTHESIA
DECEMBER 1844.

In 1894, on the fiftieth anniversary of Wells having his own tooth pulled under laughing gas, a group of American dentists placed a plaque on the building in downtown Hartford where the historic event took place. The building is now a restaurant, but it still has the plaque, which reads:

TO THE MEMORY OF HORACE WELLS, DENTIST, WHO UPON THIS SPOT DECEMBER 11, 1844 SUBMITTED TO A SURGICAL OPERATION, DISCOVERED, DEMONSTRATED, AND PROCLAIMED THE BLESSINGS OF ANESTHESIA.

There was a tremendous burst of activity on Wells's behalf in 1944, the one hundredth anniversary of his first use of laughing gas. Colleges of dentistry and local chapters of the American Dental Association gave speeches, presented radio shows and plays, and sponsored essay contests in praise of Wells. The ADA also formed the Horace Wells Centenary Committee, which collected all the testimonials in a book entitled *Horace Wells Dentist, Father of Surgical Anesthesia.* All forty-eight states and the District of Columbia sent in testimonials, as did dental societies in fifteen other countries, including France, Mexico, and Brazil.

So excited did the ADA become in 1944 that, at its annual convention, it conferred an honorary award upon Wells as the discoverer of anesthesia. Since Horace and Elizabeth's only child, Charles, had died in 1909 at age sixty-nine without ever having children, no descendants remained to accept the award; so the same dentists who presented it accepted the award, and placed it in ADA headquarters in Chicago. Two years later, in 1946, the Vermont State Dental Society placed a tablet on the house where Wells was born in Hartford, Vermont. It reads: BIRTHPLACE OF HORACE WELLS DENTIST— DISCOVERER OF GENERAL ANESTHESIA 1815–1848.

The Museum of Medicine and Dentistry in Hartford, Connecticut, has a Horace Wells Room, and does all it can to promote him as the discoverer of anesthesia. Recently museum officials tried to convince the United States Postal Service to issue a 1994 Horace Wells stamp commemorating the 150th anniversary of the pulling of his wisdom tooth under laughing gas. They went so far as to send a fictitious letter, signed by Wells, explaining to the United States postmaster general why he deserved a stamp "in honor of my discovery/invention of anesthesia, the greatest single advancement in the history of medicine." But Horace's plea was in vain, for the Postal Service issued no stamp.

William Morton has been honored in many ways, too. He is the only one of the four contestants in the Hall of Fame for Great Americans, established in 1900 by New York University. When inducted in 1920, Morton joined such notables as George Washington, Abraham Lincoln, Ralph Waldo Emerson, and Samuel Morse.

The American Society of Anesthesiologists, founded in 1905, has never officially named one man or another as the discoverer. However, in 1941 the society placed a plaque at Morton's birthsite in Charlton, Massachusetts, proclaiming it the BIRTHPLACE OF WILLIAM THOMAS GREEN MORTON, 1819–1868, WHO FIRST PUBLICLY DEMONSTRATED ETHER ANESTHESIA OCTOBER 16th, 1846.

Massachusetts General Hospital remains Morton's biggest booster. Although operations are no longer performed in the Ether Dome, this operating theater has been restored to look like it did on October 16, 1846, the day of the Gilbert Abbott operation. A large plaque in the Dome describes the historic

The William Morton stamp issued by Transkei in 1984

operation and asserts that "knowledge of this discovery spread from this room throughout the civilized world and a new era for surgery began." In the vault where the old records are kept, the hospital has Morton's original inhaler, which it displays on special occasions, such as the 150th anniversary of the Gilbert Abbott operation in 1996. Since 1903, the hospital has also held Ether Day celebrations every October 16 to commemorate the Gilbert Abbott operation.

Morton was further honored in 1984 when Transkei, a small nation that broke away from South Africa in 1976, issued a beautiful twenty-five–cent stamp in his memory. But

DR. CRAWFORD W. LONG

UNITED STATES POSTAGE 2¢

The Crawford Long stamp issued by the United States in 1940

Crawford Long is the only one of the four men honored by a United States stamp. A two-cent stamp portraying him in old age went on sale in 1940.

Georgia has remembered Crawford Long in many ways. Long County near Savannah was named for him, Atlanta has a Crawford W. Long Hospital, and Athens and Jefferson are connected by the Crawford W. Long Memorial Highway. The Georgia doctor is also honored at the Crawford W. Long Museum, which opened in Jefferson in 1957. After pointing out such items as Crawford Long's chess set, medical bags, and the instrument kit he had with him the day he died, museum director Susan B. Deaver argues Long's case over Coca-Colas at the nearby Crawford W. Long Pharmacy. "If the definition of a discovery is being the first to make use of a new process," says Deaver, "then Dr. Crawford Long was the one who discovered anesthesia." The Crawford W. Long Museum in Jefferson also holds a yearly event in Long's honor around the time of his birthday, November 1. The Crawford W. Long Days festival features demonstrations of nineteenth-century crafts and children's games, as well as storytelling and other entertainment typical of Dr. Long's time.

Crawford Long has another unique honor among the four contenders. Each state is allowed to have statues of two people in the United States Capitol in Washington, D.C. Georgia chose Crawford Long and Confederate vice president Alexander Stephens. When their statues were completed in the 1920s, the two old University of Georgia roommates were reunited in the nation's Capitol. The Long statue says on its pedestal: GEORGIA'S TRIBUTE: CRAWFORD W. LONG, M.D., DISCOVERER OF THE USE OF ETHER AS AN ANESTHETIC IN SURGERY ON MARCH 30th, 1842, AT JEFFERSON, JACKSON COUNTY, GEORGIA, U.S.A. "MY PROFESSION IS TO ME A MINISTRY FROM GOD."

The only major reminder of Jackson—his childhood home in Plymouth—is now headquarters for the Mayflower Society, an organization that perpetuates the memory of the Pilgrims. In the parlor where Ralph Waldo Emerson married Jackson's sister Lydia is the rocking chair in which Jackson claimed to have etherized himself after breathing the model-volcano fumes. "Seated in this chair Dr. Charles T. Jackson discovered etherization February 1842," claims the inscription, which was written by Edward Waldo Emerson, Jackson's nephew. About the only people today who believe these words are the women who work at the Mayflower Society. They tell visitors who ask about the house, "The inventor of anesthesia lived here."

Now and then there have been clashes in the twentieth century among backers of the four men. In 1937 Georgia officials banned a textbook from their schools because they felt it gave too little credit to Long and too much to Morton. Newspapers published a photograph of Georgia governor Eurith Rivers ripping up the textbook under the caption "Second War Between the States."

At about the same time, Hollywood decided to make a movie emphasizing Morton's role in the discovery. The Georgia Senate's response was to adopt a resolution calling the proposed film a hoax upon the public. More trouble came from Horace Wells boosters, who wanted the studio to make a movie about *their* man instead. The making of the movie proved to be much like Morton's fruitless quest for the $100,000. The story was bumped from one scriptwriter and director to another and took six years to produce. In an effort to avoid controversy, the studio ended up turning the story into a light comedy called *The Great Moment*. Reviewers wrote that the 1944 film was an "incoherent mess," "funny if you can enjoy laughter in contexts of physical misery," and "more in bad taste than in good humor."

From time to time we authors revive the controversy, too, often viewing it in startlingly different ways, depending on our viewpoints. Long supporters commonly claim that he was too busy to write an article, while a Morton admirer accuses Long of having "plenty of leisure for archery or croquet," but not enough intelligence to recognize a great discovery. Wells is "sensitive" and "shy" to his followers, but "lacked persistence" in the eyes of an author favoring Morton. Most authors view Jackson as a "thief of glory" as one phrased it, yet a rare Jackson defender portrays him as an innocent soul forever being taken advantage of by others.

Perhaps the wisest final verdict is that of Dr. J. Marion Sims, who felt that all four men deserve at least some of the credit. If we think of a discoverer as the first person to use a

Right: This portrait at the International Museum of Surgical Science in Chicago is one of the few places in which (from left) Wells, Long, Jackson, and Morton appear together.

new process, then Susan B. Deaver is right—Crawford Long was the discoverer. Unquestionably Horace Wells was the first to make widespread use of anesthesia in a populous area, and he also blazed the way for the Boston doctors to be more receptive toward the next demonstrator who came along. That man, William Morton, deserves a world of credit, too, for he made anesthesia an accepted part of medicine. As for Charles Jackson, he destroyed his credibility by claiming other discoveries, yet it is undeniable that his suggestions played a key role in Morton's success.

The monument most in keeping with the view that the credit should be shared was placed in Boston's Public Garden in 1867. The Ether Monument, as it is called, honors the discovery of anesthesia, without crediting anyone for it. Oliver Wendell Holmes, who coined the word *anesthesia,* quipped that this monument should be inscribed "TO E(I)THER."

But there is a much more meaningful monument to the four men—one that is reenacted around the world each day. For many years after the discovery of anesthesia, thousands of surgical patients continued to die for reasons that mystified doctors. Then in the 1870s scientists discovered that germs were the culprits. In the late 1800s antiseptic surgery, which involves killing germs, and aseptic surgery, which involves keeping them out of the operating room in the first place, were introduced. These new methods enabled anesthesia to achieve its full potential, for deaths from germs had held back surgery nearly as much as the threat of pain.

The combination of anesthesia and germ-free surgery allowed doctors to do increasingly complex operations, and to conquer conditions that had once been considered hopeless. Doctors learned to operate on the brain, to remove cancerous tumors from deep within the body, and even to remove a patient's heart and transplant another in its place. At the same time, new and better anesthetics were discovered.

Each year in the United States, more than 20 million sur-

The Ether Monument in Boston's Public Garden

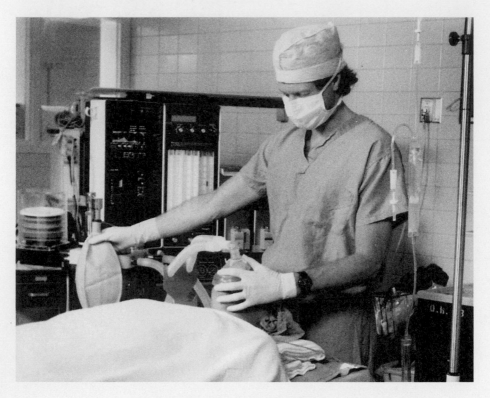

An anesthesiologist of today

gical procedures are performed that require anesthesia. For the entire world, the figure is in the hundreds of millions. It is the rare person who goes through life without ever needing an anesthetic. All of us who have enjoyed the blessings of anesthesia are the ultimate tribute to Long, Wells, Jackson, and Morton, for we are their living memorials.

BIBLIOGRAPHY

Boland, Frank Kells. *The First Anesthetic: The Story of Crawford Long*. Athens, Georgia: University of Georgia Press, 1950.

Galas, Judith C. *Anesthetics: Surgery without Pain*. San Diego: Lucent Books, 1992.

Gies, William J., editor. *Horace Wells Dentist, Father of Surgical Anesthesia*. Hartford: Horace Wells Centenary Committee, 1948.

Jacobs, Joseph. *Dr. Crawford W. Long: The Distinguished Physician-Pharmacist*. Atlanta, 1919.

Long, Crawford W., *An Account of the First Use of Sulfuric Ether* (1849), and Sims, J. Marion, *The Discovery of Anesthesia* (1877). Park Ridge, Illinois: The Wood Library-Museum of Anesthesiology (Reprint Series), 1992.

Ludovici, L. J. *The Discovery of Anesthesia*. New York: Thomas Y. Crowell Company, 1962.

MacQuitty, Betty. *Victory over Pain: Morton's Discovery of Anesthesia*. New York: Taplinger Publishing Company, 1971.

Raper, Howard Riley. *Man against Pain: The Epic of Anesthesia*. New York: Prentice-Hall, 1945.

Robinson, Victor. *Victory over Pain: A History of Anesthesia*. New York: Henry Schuman, 1946.

Seeman, Bernard. *Man against Pain*. Philadelphia and New York: Chilton Books, 1962.

Shapiro, Irwin. *The Gift of Magic Sleep: Early Experiments in Anesthesia*. New York: Coward, McCann & Geoghegan, 1979.

Taylor, Frances Long. *Crawford W. Long and the Discovery of Ether Anesthesia*. New York: Paul B. Hoeber, Inc., 1928.

Wolfe, Richard J., and Menczer, Leonard F., editors. *I Awaken to Glory*. Boston: Boston Medical Library in the Francis A. Countway Library of Medicine, 1994.

PHOTO CREDITS

INDEX